# *Two for the Seesaw*

## A COMEDY-DRAMA IN THREE ACTS

### *By William Gibson*

S A M U E L   F R E N C H ,   I N C .
25 WEST 45TH STREET             NEW YORK 10036
7623 SUNSET BOULEVARD        HOLLYWOOD 90046
*LONDON*                                      *TORONTO*

## TWO FOR THE SEESAW

Presented by Fred Coe at the Booth Theatre, New York City, January 16, 1958. Staged by Arthur Penn; setting and lighting by George Jenkins; costumes by Virginia Volland; production stage manager, Porter Van Zandt.

## THE CAST

JERRY RYAN.........................*Henry Fonda*
GITTEL MOSCA......................*Anne Bancroft*

The action takes place this past year, between fall and spring, in two rooms—Jerry's and Gittel's—in New York City.

## *ACT ONE*

SCENE 1: *Both rooms. September, late afternoon.*
SCENE 2: *Gittel's room. Midnight, the same day.*
SCENE 3: *Both rooms. Daybreak following.*

## *ACT TWO*

SCENE 1: *Jerry's room. October, dusk.*
SCENE 2: *Both rooms. December, noon.*
SCENE 3: *Gittel's room. February, a Saturday night.*

## *ACT THREE*

SCENE 1: *Gittel's room. March, midday.*
SCENE 2: *Jerry's room. May, dusk.*
SCENE 3: *Both rooms. A few days later, afternoon.*

# SETTING

The set consists of two rooms, angled toward each other, but in no way related; they are in different buildings, a few miles apart, in New York.

The room on Stage Right is Jerry Ryan's and is the tiny living-room of a bleak two-room flat in a lower East Side tenement. It contains principally a narrow couch with a kitchen chair at its side, and at the beginning has the depressing air of having been moved into recently and minimally; the telephone, for instance, sits on the bare floor. In the Right wall is a window through which we see nearby rooftops. In the rear wall is a doorway which opens into a kitchen so dark it is practically indecipherable; in this kitchen are a gas range, a covered bathtub, and the entrance-door of the flat. The Left wall of the room towards Stage Center is omitted or fragmented, so as not to obstruct our view of the other room on the stage.

The room on Stage Left is Gittel Mosca's, and is the living-room of a flat in a run-down brownstone in midtown. It is on a lower level than Jerry's, is larger and lighter, and has a pleasantly untidy and cluttered air of having been lived in for some time; though furnished in very ordinary taste, it speaks of human comfort and warmth. Downstage in the Left wall is the entrance-door, and Upstage a doorway into the kitchen, which is partly visible. The room contains among other things a studio double-bed, a night-table with lamp and phone, a bureau, chairs, and a dress-dummy and sewing-machine in the corner; there is also a window which looks out upon the street.

NOTE: Following instructions from the author, this play may be released only to amateur groups at which the audience is non-segregated.

4

# Two for the Seesaw

## ACT ONE

### Scene 1

*Both rooms.*

*It is a late afternoon in September; the windows of both rooms are open, and the sounds of TRAFFIC float in. Gittel's room is empty.*

*In the other room* JERRY *is sitting on his couch, cigarette in hand, searching with his finger down the phonebook open between his feet.* JERRY *is a long fellow in his thirties, attractive, with an underlayer of melancholy and, deeper, a lurking anger; his manner of dress, which is casually conservative, is too prosperous for this drab and disorderly room. The couch is unmade, the kitchen chair next to it has a typewriter on it and is hung with clothes, a handsome suitcase is open on the unswept floor, and the dust is gathering in bunches along the wall-board. Now* JERRY *finds the number he wants, and dials. The PHONE in Gittel's room rings. On the fourth ring* JERRY *hangs up. Simultaneously there has been a rattle of key and knob at Gittel's door;* GITTEL *runs in, not stopping to set down her bag of groceries, and grabs the phone.*

GITTEL. (*Out of breath.*) Yeah, hello? (*She waits a second.*) Oh, hell. (*She hangs up. She is a dark thin girl of indeterminate age, too eccentric to be called pretty, nervous, uncouth, and engaging by virtue of some indestructible cheerfulness in her; all her clothes—denim skirt, peasant blouse, sandals—are somehow misfits, and*

5

*everything she does has the jerky and lightweight intensity of a bird on the ground.)*

(*Now she and* JERRY *go about their separate business.* JERRY *lifts the suitcase onto the couch, and taking out his clothes—a fine jacket, a fine suit, a fine topcoat—begins hanging them on a clothes-rod set catty-corner between two walls; while he is putting some shoes down, the rod slips out of one support and everything falls on his head.)*

JERRY. Oh, you son of a bitch. (*He lets it all lie, and returns into the kitchen. He comes back with a block of wood, hammer, and nails; he nails the block any which way under the socket on one wall, puts the rod back in place, and hangs the clothes up again; this time the rod holds.)*

(*Meanwhile* GITTEL, *on her way to the kitchen with her bag of groceries, has stopped in front of the dress-dummy and looks critically at a gaudy bodice pinned together on it; she stands unmoving for a minute, then with her free hand unpins the collar and commences to work. After a while she steps back, and is disgusted.)*

GITTEL. Oh, for Christ sakes. (*She gives up, slaps the pins down, and continues on to the kitchen, where we see her pour out a panful of milk and set it to warm on a gas-burner; she puts the other groceries away in cupboard and ice-box.* JERRY *finishes with his clothes, turns to regard the phone, sits on the couch, checks the same number, and dials it once more. The PHONE in Gittel's room rings.* GITTEL *runs back and answers it just as* JERRY *is about to hang up after two rings.)* Yeah, hello?

JERRY. (*His voice when we hear it now is well-educated, with a dead-pan mockery in it that is essentially detached.)* Gittel Mosca, please.

GITTEL. It's me, who's this?

JERRY. This is Jerry Ryan. We met across eight or nine unidentified bodies last night at Oscar's. I'm a slight acquaintance of his from back home.

GITTEL. Oh?

JERRY. I say slight, about 170 pounds. Six one. (*Waits; then elaborately*) Red beard—

GITTEL. Oh, you were the fella in the dark hat that didn't say anything!

JERRY. You must know some very bright hats. I overheard you talk about a frigidaire you want to sell. Be all right if I stop by for a look?

GITTEL. At that frigidaire?

JERRY. It's all I had in mind, to begin with.

GITTEL. It's not a frigidaire, it's an ice-box.

JERRY. Good enough. No electric bill, a product of American know-how. I could be there in about—

GITTEL. I gave it away!

JERRY. (*A pause, stymied.*) Oh. Not very kind of you.

GITTEL. I just helped him lug it home. Some jerk I never saw in my life, Sophie sent him over, so I let him have it just to get rid of the goddam thing. Why didn't you ask me last night?

JERRY. I didn't want to be among the quick. Last night.

GITTEL. Huh?

JERRY. I changed my mind and life today, great day. I thought I'd start by putting my nose in on you for a look.

GITTEL. It just isn't here.

JERRY. So you said. (*A pause, both waiting.*) Yes. Thanks anyway.

GITTEL. Sure. (JERRY *hangs up.*) Oh, hell.

(*She hangs up too.* JERRY *after a morose moment gets up, fingers in his pack of cigarettes, finds it empty. En route to the window with it he bumps his knee against the couch; he lifts his foot and shoves it back, it jars the wall, the clothes-rod is jogged out of the other support, and the clothes fall on the floor.*)

JERRY. Agh, you son of a bitch!

*(He grabs the rod and brings it down over his knee; it only bends, flies up in his· face. He attacks it again, can't break it, trips over it, and doesn't know where to get rid of it, in a rage which is comic, until suddenly he throws a short punch into the window, not comic; the glass flies. He stands, grimly considers his fist, his surroundings, his state of mind, gets away from the window, walks into the phone on the floor, regards it, gathers it up, and dials. Meanwhile* GITTEL'S *milk boils over as she is removing her sandals. She jumps up, and is hurrying toward the kitchen when her PHONE rings.)*

GITTEL. Oh, for Christ sakes. *(She is undecided, then hurries back and grabs up the phone.)* Just a minute, will you, I'm boiling over. *(She lays it down, hurries into the kitchen, turns the milk off, and comes back to the phone.)* Milk all over the goddam stove, yeah? *(*JERRY *sits with his eyes closed, the mouthpiece against his eyebrows.)* Hello? *(*JERRY *separates his face and the mouthpiece.)* Hello, is anybody on this line?

JERRY. No.

GITTEL. Huh? *(*JERRY *hangs up.)* Hey!

*(She stares at the phone in her hand, then replaces it. She decides to shrug it off and go back to her milk, which she cools off by adding more from the container; but she stands in the doorway sipping it for only a second, then makes for the phone. She dials, and waits.* JERRY *walking in his room finds his hand is bleeding a bit, wraps it in his handkerchief, and has a private argument, not liking himself.)*

JERRY. You broken-hearted fly, *begin. (He gazes around the bare room, answers himself mordantly.)* Begin what? The conquest of the Sunday Times?

(*He shoves the suitcase off the couch, lies down and extracts section after section of newspaper from under him, flinging them away.* GITTEL *gets an answer.*)

GITTEL. Sophie. Is Oscar there?—Well, listen, that hat-type friend of his last night, the long one, what's his number?—Look, girl, will you drag your mind up out of your girdle and go see if Oscar's got it written down?

JERRY. (*His legs are overhanging, he moves back, but now his head bumps the wall. He gets to his feet and considers the couch grimly, muttering:*) Six feet of man, five feet of couch, calls for a new man.

(*He stands the suitcase on end at the couch foot, lies down again with his feet out upon it, and extracts and flings away a final section of newspaper.* GITTEL *scribbles.*)

GITTEL. 69 what? Yeah, yeah, yeah, very funny.

(*She clicks down, and immediately dials it.* JERRY'S *PHONE rings. His head lifts to regard it, and he lets it ring another time before he leans over to pick it up.*)

JERRY. (*Guardedly.*) Yes?

GITTEL. (*Quickly, a little nervous.*) Look, I been thinking here about that ice-box, what we could do is I could take you around the corner where this character lives, if you offer him a buck or two he might turn loose of it, and it's worth five easy, what do you say? (JERRY *on his elbow mulls her over.*) Hey, you still with me?

JERRY. I don't know yet, I might be against you. I'm not in the book, how did you get my number?

GITTEL. Sophie gave me it. Now about this ice-box, I mean for nothing I let this kid have a real bargain, you could afford to make it worth his while, what do you think?

JERRY. I think you can't be calling about an ice-box you had to help someone carry through the streets to get rid of.

GITTEL. What do you mean?

JERRY. You're calling either because like me you have nothing better to do, or because you're under the misap—

GITTEL. (*Indignantly.*) I got eleven different things I could be doing!

JERRY. Different isn't better, why aren't we doing them? Or because you're under the misapprehension it was me who just hung up on you.

GITTEL. (*Confused.*) Uh—it wasn't?

JERRY. Whoever it was had a reason. Question now is what's yours? If a man calls up to say he's not calling up, a girl who calls him back can be either lonely, solicitous, prying, a help or a nuisance—

GITTEL. Look, how'd I get in the wrong here?

JERRY. —and I'm curious to know which.

GITTEL. Did you call me up about this ice-box or not?

JERRY. Not.

(GITTEL *bangs the phone down, gets up, and tears her scrap of paper with his number into bits; she throws them into the waste-basket.* JERRY *after a surprised moment finds this somewhat amusing, smiles in spite of himself, clicks down, and dials back.* GITTEL'S *PHONE rings, and she comes to answer it;* JERRY'S *manner now is rather teasing.*)

GITTEL. Yeah, hello?

JERRY. I said I didn't call you about an ice-box.

GITTEL. (*Darkly.*) Whaat?

JERRY. It seems I did, but I didn't.

GITTEL. Look, I can't follow this whole conversation. You called—

JERRY. I called because the only female voice I've heard on this phone is the robot lady with the correct time, and I'm going off my nut in solitary here. I called to make contact.

GITTEL. Oh!

JERRY. With someone of the weaker sex who's weaker.

GITTEL. (*Pause.*) Okay, here I am. (JERRY *ponders it.*) Contact!

JERRY. I called to invite you to dinner tonight. And a show.

GITTEL. So why didn't you?

JERRY. I was afraid you'd say yes or no.

GITTEL. Huh? I would of said sure.

JERRY. See what I mean? All right, which show? It's Sunday, we'll have to see what—

GITTEL. Well, now I'm *not* so sure.

JERRY. Why?

GITTEL. I don't know if I want to get involved now, you sound awful complicated to me!

JERRY. How? Man calls to invite you to dinner via the ice-box, you say there isn't any ice-box, he waits to be invited in without the ice-box, you show no interest in anything but the ice-box, you call him back to invite him to invite you via the ice-box again, he expresses interest in your personality, not your ice-box, you're so devoted to the ice-box you hang up. What's complicated?

GITTEL. (*A pause.*) Look, what's your point?

JERRY. (*Dryly.*) I'm kind of pointless, how are you?

GITTEL. I mean I'm the girl, right? You're the man, make up your mind. *Then* ask me to dinner, and I'll make up my mind.

JERRY. My point is I've been trying to make up my mind for a month here.

GITTEL. What, to ask me to dinner?

JERRY. To climb off a certain piece of flypaper. It's a beginning. (*Pause.*) I mean once you break a leg in five places you hesitate to step out.

GITTEL. Oh!

JERRY. It's one night in the year I don't want to eat alone. (*Another pause.*) The reason I hung up was I didn't want to say please. Help me.

GITTEL. Well. How'd you expect to pick me up?

JERRY. How far east are you?

GITTEL. Off Second.

JERRY. I'll be there in half an hour.

GITTEL. Maybe you shouldn't, is it okay enough to?

JERRY. Is what okay enough to?

GITTEL. Your leg.

JERRY. What leg? Oh. (*He is deadpan:*) I don't know, it seems to have affected my head. I'll see you. (*He hangs up, replaces the phone on his couch. GITTEL stares, shakes her head, glances at an alarm-clock on the night-table, hangs up hurriedly, and darts out her door into the hall, where from another room we hear the bathtub WATER being turned on. Meanwhile JERRY's mood has lightened; he picks up his fallen clothes and lays them across his couch, brushes his jacket off, and slips into it. He is on his way out with his hat when the PHONE rings, and he comes back to answer it, thinking it is GITTEL and speaking dryly into the mouthpiece:*) I'm as sane as you are, stop worrying. (*Then his face changes, becomes guarded.*) Yes, this is Mr. Ry— (*His mouth sets. After a second:*) Who's calling from Omaha? (*Suddenly he hangs up. He stands over the phone, his hand upon it, until it begins to ring again; then he puts his hat on slowly, and walks out of the room. He pulls his KITCHEN LIGHT out, and leaves, closing the outer door. The PHONE continues to ring.*)

*CURTAIN*

## ACT ONE

### SCENE 2

*Gittel's room.*

*It is close to midnight the same day, and both rooms are dark, except for the LIGHTS of the city in the sky beyond their open windows. The faint SOUNDS of metropolitan night are audible. Under GITTEL's door there is a line of YELLOW LIGHT from the*

*hall, where presently we hear VOICES and FOOT-*
*STEPS; the door is unlocked, and* GITTEL *comes in*
*with* JERRY *behind her, both silhouetted. Their*
*mood is light, though* JERRY'S *manner remains*
*essentially ironic and preoccupied.*

GITTEL. Look out for the furniture. Got to be a bat to
find your way around *this* goddam room in the dark.

JERRY. Some of my best friends are bats. And the rest
are cuckoos. The— Oogh!

GITTEL. There. (*She clicks on a LAMP, which gives a*
*cozy light, and tosses her purse and a theatre-program on*
*the bed.* JERRY *is holding a carton of cokes and a bag,*
*and rubbing his shin with his bandaged hand;* GITTEL
*comes back, grinning.*) So whyn't you listen?

JERRY. (*Surrenders the things.*) No place like home,
be it ever so deadly. Sixty per cent of the accidents in
this country occur in the home. (GITTEL *takes the things*
*into her kitchen.*) Doesn't include ruptured marriages.
Be safe, be homeless.

GITTEL. (*Calling in, amused.*) What'll you have, coke
or beer, Jerry?

JERRY. Anything you're having that's wet.

GITTEL. I'm having warm milk.

JERRY. (*With doubt.*) Warm milk. (*He considers it,*
*putting his hat on the dress-dummy while* GITTEL *in*
*the kitchen lights the gas under a potful.*) I think I'm
too old for you. I'll have a hell-bent coke.

GITTEL. Coke's got caffeine in it, maybe I'll give you a
beer better, huh?

JERRY. Better for what?

GITTEL. It's more relaxing. You had three cups of
coffee at dinner, a coke now makes—

JERRY. Gittel, call off the St. Bernards. I mean let's
not nurse me, I've been taken care of to shreds. (GITTEL
*is brought back to the doorway by his tone, which has an*
*edge.*) Coke, and damn the torpedoes.

GITTEL. You said you don't sleep. So you *won't* sleep.

(*She goes back into the kitchen.* JERRY *thinks it over, dryly.*)

JERRY. It's a non-income-producing habit. If you guarantee I'll sleep with beer, you can give me beer.

GITTEL. (*Comes back into the doorway.*) Look, let's start all over, on your own. Coke or beer?

JERRY. Warm milk.

GITTEL. Now listen—

JERRY. If I'm relaxing I don't want to be *casual* about it.

(GITTEL *shaking her head goes back into the kitchen; she continues from there, while* JERRY *explores the room.*)

GITTEL. What kind of bed you got you don't sleep?

JERRY. A couch I got at the Salvation Army, eight dollars.

GITTEL. Well, my God, no wonder! Take a feel of that bed. (*She comes into the doorway, points with a mug;* JERRY *stops to eye the bed.*) You know how much I paid for that mattress alone? Fifty-nine bucks! Sears' best.

JERRY. Six lovely feet long and wide enough for two, isn't it?

GITTEL. Yeah, well, that's one thing I'd never be without is a good bed, you just got to get yourself a good bed. (*She goes back into the kitchen.*) I mean figure it out, you're in it a third of your life.

JERRY. (*Dryly.*) You lead a very puritanical life, by that estimate.

GITTEL. How come? Oh. Okay, half.

JERRY. (*Interested.*) Hm. Well, I've been spending most of my nights here on the jewel-like bridges. I can't afford fifty-nine dollars just to make my bedbugs comfy.

GITTEL. You got bedbugs? (*She comes in frowning, with a box of cookies and two mugs of milk, and hands him one.*)

JERRY. Among other things eating me at night.

GITTEL. You out of work, Jerry?

JERRY. (*Inspecting his milk.*) I know why I'm drinking
this, why are you?

GITTEL. Oh, I got an ulcer. (*She indicates her chest,
explains.*) In the duodenum.

JERRY. Serious? (GITTEL *shrugging, wags her head,
makes herself comfortable on the bed, her legs under
her.*) I thought ulcers in women went out with the bicycle
built for two, isn't it a man's disease nowadays?

GITTEL. (*Philosophically.*) Well, I got it!

JERRY. Well, which are you, the old-fashioned type or
the manly type?

GITTEL. Why, what's the difference?

JERRY. Present difference might be whether I drink
this and go, or stay all night.

(*He cocks an eye at her, and* GITTEL *eyes him back
unperturbed, a moment of frank speculation, both
ways.*)

GITTEL. You don't exactly lead up to things, do you?

JERRY. Oh, I've been *up* for hours, pawing the ground.
The only question is which way to run. (*He moves away
from this subject, which leaves her perplexed; he stops
to regard the gaudy bodice on the dress-dummy, his
manner dry and light.*) Speaking of blind as a bat, who
is this for?

GITTEL. Dance costume, some kid she's at the Educa-
tion Alliance next Sunday.

JERRY. Has no bottom part, this kid she has no bottom
parts?

GITTEL. Goes with tights, natch!

JERRY. (*At the sewing machine.*) Good idea. And here
you earn an immodest living, hm?

GITTEL. (*Dubiously.*) Mmm. Half and half.

JERRY. Why, what's the other half?

GITTEL. The other half I'm unemployed!

JERRY. (*At photos on a wall.*) Well, the answer is

simple, longer costumes. Aha, acrobats. Who's the black beauty with cramps?

GITTEL. That's me.

JERRY. You?

GITTEL. Yeah, don't act so surprised! I'm dancing.

JERRY. Oh. Yes, I see. I had the impression you'd given up that line of work, or vice versa.

GITTEL. (*Indignant.*) No! That's what I *am*. Ye gods, I studied with Jose for years.

JERRY. Jose who?

GITTEL. (*Staring.*) Are you serious?

JERRY. Good question. You mean this is the real you.

GITTEL. Well, if it isn't I sure wasted a lot of seven-fifties a week!

JERRY. And Mr. America here would be your ex-mistake?

GITTEL. Who?

JERRY. Your husband.

GITTEL. Nah, Wally wasn't around long enough to *snap* a picture. That's Larry.

JERRY. (*Sagely.*) Oh. The present mistake. (*He contemplates the photos.*) Somehow there's more *of* the real you. Do you have such nice legs?

GITTEL. Sure! Well, I mean I did, but that's some time back, before I got sick, I lost a lot of weight since then.

JERRY. (*On tiptoe at one photo's neckline.*) With your old-fashioned duodenum? Can almost make it out in this one—

GITTEL. No, ulcers you put *on* weight. That diet, ye gods, six meals a day, the last hemorrhage I had I put on eighteen pounds. I looked very good. (JERRY *turns to her with a frown.*) Everybody said!

JERRY. The last.

GITTEL. Yeah, I hope it's the last. I got just so much blood!

JERRY. It is serious. How many hemorrhages have you had?

GITTEL. Two. Then when I never looked healthier in my life, they had to operate on me.

JERRY. For the ulcer?

GITTEL. Appendicitis! (*She becomes self-conscious under his continued gaze; she laughs.*) No kidding, I'm a physical wreck, practically.

JERRY. (*After a moment, raises his milk to her.*) To your physique. As is, without appendix. I couldn't resist another ounce.

(*He drinks to her, and* GITTEL *cheerfully acknowledges it with a sip of her own.*)

GITTEL. So okay, that's what's wrong with me, what's wrong with you?

JERRY. Me? Not a thing.

GITTEL. How'd you break your leg in five places?

JERRY. Oh, my leg. It broke with grief. (*He empties the mug, sets it down, stops at her RADIO and clicks it on, sees that it lights up, clicks it off, and moves on, taking out a cigar.*)

GITTEL. Look, whyn't you settle down and rest up? (JERRY *turns to her, she anticipates him.*) I'm not nursing, it just makes me nervous to watch!

JERRY. (*Dryly.*) I have two rates of motion, the other is collapse. The last lady who invited me to settle down I couldn't get up for nine years. (*He drops in a chair apart from her, unwrapping the cigar;* GITTEL *stares.*)

GITTEL. Who was that?

JERRY. Her name escapes me. The question at hand is how we're to make up our mind.

GITTEL. About what?

JERRY. About my staying over. I appreciate the invitation, but I'm not sure you should insist. On the other hand, it's very pleasant here and I can't plead any prior engagements.

GITTEL. (*A pause.*) I don't get you, Jerry.

JERRY. I only sound hard to get. No one's had much trouble.

GITTEL. I mean first you can't say if you even want to eat with me, the next minute, bing, into bed. Only it's all talk, how come?

JERRY. It's exploratory talk. Like the old lady who said how do I know what I think till I hear what I say.

GITTEL. Ahuh. Is that the way you decide everything?

JERRY. How?

GITTEL. In your head?

JERRY. Well, I have a little gray thingamajig in here supposed to save me false moves. Where do you decide things?

GITTEL. Well, that one not in my head! I mean a couple of false moves might get you further.

JERRY. (*Studies her for a moment.*) Don't rush me. I think I should examine what I'm getting into.

GITTEL. (*Eyebrows up.*) Who said yes, yet?

JERRY. And so should you. What if all I can afford is a— (*He waves a hand at the photos.*) lady on a picture, not a whole human being with hemorrhages and so on?

GITTEL. (*Indignantly.*) So who's giving them to you?

JERRY. Well. I'm burning my bridges before me. Maybe we could have a little music to obscure the future, I've missed that, too.

GITTEL. My God, you haven't got a radio even?

JERRY. No, why?

GITTEL. Everybody's got a radio! (*He lights the cigar.* GITTEL *stares at him, till the RADIO comes in under her hand; she dials around to some music.*) Listen, are you really broke?

JERRY. (*Inspecting the cigar.*) What kind of a name is Gittel? Has an exotic ring, Eskimo or—

GITTEL. Polish. Are you?

JERRY. Polish?

GITTEL. Broke!

JERRY. Why do you ask?

GITTEL. I just want to know if that's what keeping you up nights, and if so what'd we eat out and go to a show for? I mean we could of gone Dutch at least.

JERRY. (*Deadpan.*) I thought you were Italian.

GITTEL. Who, me? Jewish!

JERRY. Mosca?

GITTEL. Oh, *that's* exotic. It's my stage name.

JERRY. What stage are you in?

GITTEL. Huh?

JERRY. What's your real name?

GITTEL. Too long. For the marquees, Moscowitz.

JERRY. So you became a witzless Italian. Is that where you were born?

GITTEL. Italy?

JERRY. Poland.

GITTEL. (*Indignantly.*) I was born in the Bronx. Listen, whyn't you get unemployed insurance? It's what I do.

JERRY. Well. For one thing, I'm not a legal resident of this state.

GITTEL. Oh. (*She considers it.*) So what state are you from, legally?

JERRY. Nebraska.

GITTEL. Nebraska. That's somewhere way out in California, isn't it?

JERRY. I think it's Nevada that's in California.

GITTEL. I mean, you're a long ways from home. You don't know anybody here you can borrow from?

JERRY. (*In his chair, appraises her steadily.*) Only you.

(*A quiet moment, their eyes not leaving each other.*
    GITTEL *then picks up his mug, to refill it, debating.*)

GITTEL. How much do you need?

JERRY. (*Eyes down.*) You're a very generous girl. (*Then he gets to his feet, his voice flattening; he walks away from her.*) Much too generous. Don't play the fairy godmother, the wolf will eat you up.

GITTEL. You said you were broke!

JERRY. No, you said I was broke. The unromantic fact is that last year I made fifteen thousand dollars.

GITTEL. (*Staring.*) Doing what?

JERRY. I'm an attorney.

GITTEL. You mean a lawyer?

JERRY. Attorney. To be exotic.

GITTEL. (*Indignant*.) I got eighteen bucks to get me through the month, what am I helping you out for?

JERRY. (*Indifferent, at the window.*) Offhand I think you enjoy feeding stray wolves.

GITTEL. What?

JERRY. I think you're a born victim.

GITTEL. Of who?

JERRY. Yourself.

GITTEL. (*Staring.*) Am I wrong or have you got a nerve? I felt sorry for you, what's so terrible?

JERRY. (*Turning.*) For me.

GITTEL. Sure.

JERRY. How old are you?

GITTEL. Twenty-nine, so?

JERRY. So. Don't talk like twenty-eight. At thirty you're over the hill, half a life gone, there's very little in this room to show for it. I think it's time you worried about your worries.

GITTEL. (*Scowling.*) I do! I got plans!

JERRY. What plans?

GITTEL. Several! I'm starting right away with this Larry, we're going to work up a whole goddam dance recital, why shouldn't we be the new Humphrey and Weidman? I'm hunting everywhere for a cheap loft to fix up a studio, I can rent it out for classes too. Not to mention I'll probably do the costumes for a show downtown, Oscar's in a new theatre bunch there, he says he can—

JERRY (*Flatly.*) None of this will happen. (*This is true enough to take the wind out of* GITTEL *for a moment.*)

GITTEL. (*Incensed.*) So I'll think up something else! Why are you riding me for?

JERRY. Seriously?

GITTEL. Yeah!

JERRY. (*Evenly.*) Because I enjoy you, life is short, and if you're spending it like a sailor on a spree you might as well spend some on me, but all I probably mean is trouble, I can be here today and gone tomorrow, and

I'd rather not be responsible for an ingenuous little nit-wit like you. In one word.

GITTEL. (*Scowling.*) What's ingenuous mean, smart?

JERRY. Dumb. Naïve.

GITTEL. Oh, for Christ sakes. I had a room of my own in the Village at sixteen, what do you think, to play potsy? All those reasons, I think you're just scared!

JERRY. (*A pause, levelly.*) Do you sleep with him?

GITTEL. Who?

JERRY. Mr. America. Larry.

GITTEL. He's a *dancer.*

JERRY. So you said.

GITTEL. I mean we're very good friends and all that, but my God. You think I'm peculiar or something? (*Her eyes widen.*) Are you?

JERRY. Am I what?

GITTEL. Queer?

JERRY. (*A pause, shakes his head.*) Oh, you've gone too far. (*He puts down the cigar.*) No one's in your life now?

GITTEL. No, I'm free as a bird, goddam it.

JERRY. I'm free as a worm. We can keep it as simple as that, an item of diet.

(*His hands gesture for her, and* GITTEL *readily comes;* JERRY *kisses her. It begins temperately enough, but as* GITTEL *cooperates it becomes a whole-hearted and protracted undertaking. It is* GITTEL *who slides out of it, leaving* JERRY *with his hands trembling; she is a bit jittery herself.*)

GITTEL. Brother. How long you been on the wagon?

JERRY. A year.

GITTEL. (*Staring.*) Where you been, in jail? (JERRY *reaches, grasping her arms this time inexorably. He kisses her again; she resists weakly, responds, resists very weakly, and gives up, hanging loosely in his hands until they part mouths for air.*) Look, let's not get all worked up if we're not going to finish it, huh?

JERRY. Who's not going to, huh?

GITTEL. I mean you just have another cookie to calm down, and then maybe you better go.

JERRY. Go!

GITTEL. Please.

JERRY. (*Releases her. A silence.*) Is that what you meant by a false move would get me further?

GITTEL. No, I—

JERRY. Go where? (*He turns away, very annoyed, finds himself at the radio, and mocks her:*) Back to a room without a radio?

GITTEL. (*Weakly.*) Radio costs nineteen ninety-five—

JERRY. That's cheap enough. I had the impression you'd been inviting me all night. To buy a radio? (*He snaps the RADIO off, and walks.*)

GITTEL. (*Defensive.*) I got an iron-clad rule I wouldn't sleep with God Almighty on the first date, you want me to be *promiscuous?* In the second place you—walk around too much— (*She works up some indignation.*) —and in the third place I can't stand cigars in the first place, and in the fourth place I tell you my whole life practically and what do I hear out of you, no news at all, why should I hit the hay right away with someone I don't know if he's—

JERRY. (*Wheels on her so bitingly it stops her like a blow.*) *Because I'm drowning in cement here!*

GITTEL. Where?

JERRY. This town! (*He paces, talking through his teeth, more to himself than to her.*) I haven't passed a word with a living soul for a month, until I called Oscar —and we never liked one another! Everyone else I knew here has moved to Connecticut, Vermont, the Arctic Circle. I've worn out a pair of shoes in the museums. And a pair of pants in bad movies. And if I hike over another beautiful bridge here by my lonesome, so help me, I'll jump off! So I go back to my cell, twenty-one dollars a month, with garbage-pails in the hall they'll find me gassed to death by some morning. (*He turns on her.*) And I can't *spend* nineteen ninety-five on a radio!

GITTEL. (*The neighbors.*) Sssh! Why?

JERRY. (*Hissing.*) Because I came east with five hundred dollars. I'm living on three-fifty a day here now.

GITTEL. (*Hissing.*) You spent about sixteen-eighty on me tonight!

JERRY. (*Hissing.*) I splurged.

GITTEL. What, on me?

JERRY. On me. I was thirty-three years old today. (GITTEL *is speechless. He lifts up his cigar, dourly.*) So, I bought myself a dollar cigar.

GITTEL. It's your *birthday?*

JERRY. Sorry it—exploded. (*He crushes it out in the ash-tray.*)

GITTEL. (*Alarmed.*) So don't ruin it! You got to buy yourself a present on your birthday, my God? Whyn't you tell me?

JERRY. Why, you'd like to give me one?

GITTEL. Sure!

JERRY. Thank you. (*He retrieves his hat from the dummy.*) I'm not hinting for handouts, from crackpot lovable waifs. Just don't tell a man go when you've been indicating come all night, it's not ladylike. (*He walks toward the door.*)

GITTEL. (*Stung.*) So what do you think you been doing right along?

JERRY. (*Stops.*) What?

GITTEL. Hinting for handouts! It's what *you* been doing all night!

JERRY. Are you talking to me?

GITTEL. Sure. All these hints, unhappy, bedbugs, broke—

JERRY. Unhappy bedbugs!

GITTEL. Unhappy! Bedbugs!

JERRY. What in God's name are you dreaming—

GITTEL. Like this minute, if I don't sleep with you they'll find you dead?

JERRY. (*Astonished.*) Who said that?

GITTEL. You did. With the garbage?

JERRY. Oh, cut it out. I—

GITTEL. Or off a bridge, you're so lonely? That's the *last* thing you said?

JERRY. I was—I— (*But he breaks off, staring at her in less disbelief.*) That was—campaign oratory. You call that all night?

GITTEL. The *first* thing said was help me. On the phone. Right?

JERRY. (*Stares, almost speechless, though he makes one more convictionless try.*) I—said I *wouldn't* say that, I—

GITTEL. Oh, come on! You said help me, I said sure. (JERRY *cannot remove his eyes from her, at a loss for words.*) I'm not complaining, I'm used to all kinds, but what do you call me names, you want it both ways? (JERRY *still stares at her, but something has opened in him that now takes him away from her, Downstage, his fingers at his brow, almost in a daze.* GITTEL *becomes concerned.*) Hey. I say something hurt your feelings?

JERRY. (*With an effort.*) Yes, slightly. I— (*He shakes his head, abandons the attempt at irony. Low:*) I'm remembering. Something from— (*It comes from far away, his tone now simple and vulnerable.*)—thirteen years ago yesterday. I was walking across the campus of Nebraska U, with a beautiful auburn-haired girl whose father was a sizeable wheel in the state. The girl and I were—intimate that summer, and I was telling her I'd have to leave school, no family to help me. The next day—my birthday—was the luckiest in my life, I got the George Norris scholarship. It kept me in school, and I became a lawyer. The girl and I—continued. (*He stops.* GITTEL *waits.*)

GITTEL. That's the whole story?

JERRY. I married her.

GITTEL. (*Darkly.*) You got a *wife?*

JERRY. Had a wife. She's divorcing me out there.

GITTEL. (*Contrite.*) Oh. You too, huh?

JERRY. Me, too. It was just before we married I learned that Lucian—her father—had wangled that scholarship for me. You know what I said?

GITTEL. What?

JERRY. Nothing. (*He opens his hands, helplessly.*) It's absolutely true, the—point you made, you made your point.

GITTEL. Which?

JERRY. I ask for handouts. I never *saw* it happening before, right under my nose. (*He shakes his head, finds his hat again, and walks once more to the door.*)

GITTEL. So where you going now?

JERRY. Back to solitary. (*Beset.*) There I go again!

GITTEL. So don't. Ye gods, if you hate it so much you don't want to go back there on your birthday, stay over. I got a couch in the back room, you take the bed. Maybe a good night's sleep you'll feel better in the morning, huh? (JERRY *stares unseeing.*) You want to stay?

JERRY. Stay?

GITTEL. So you'll get a good night's sleep. You'll feel better in the morning.

JERRY. You mean, put you out?

GITTEL. It's not out, I fit that couch. I mean you got— long legs, you know?

JERRY. Yes. (GITTEL *is eyeing his legs, with interest. When their eyes meet, it is as though for the first time, really: something warmer passes between them, they are both shy about it.*) Both of them.

GITTEL. Yeah, well, I— You mind my sheets? (*She yanks the bedspread down, takes a pillow, gathers things up.*) I put them on clean yesterday and I had a bath.

JERRY. No. It's kind of you to offer, kind of absurd, but kind—

GITTEL. What do you mean absurd? You got a lousy bed, tomorrow you'll get some kerosene and see where they come out of the wall.

JERRY. Gittel. You're a very sweet girl—

GITTEL. (*Embarrassed.*) Well—you're a very sweet girl, too. The john's right out there behind you—

JERRY. —but all I proposed was a change of bedmates.

GITTEL. Listen, all *I* got in mind is a good night's sleep you'll feel better in the morning—

JERRY. (*Simultaneously with her.*) —feel better in the morning. No doubt.

GITTEL. (*All settled.*) So okay! (*She turns with her armful into the kitchen, puts out the LIGHT there.*)

JERRY. Gittel!

GITTEL. (*Within.*) What?

JERRY. I can't.

GITTEL. (*Within.*) I'm all packed!

JERRY. (*A pause.*) Crazy. (*Nevertheless, the bed attracts his eye; he turns back from it.*) Gittel! (GITTEL *reappears, still with her armful.*) Look, agree with me. It would be an act of—frailty to stay after—

GITTEL. What, on your birthday? (*She goes back in.* JERRY *considers this argument for a long moment, contemplates the bed, and the room around it, and sighs.*)

JERRY. Gittel. (GITTEL *reappears; his tone is humble.*) Should I really stay?

GITTEL. Look, don't nudya me! You want to stay?

JERRY. (*A pause.*) I haven't been in a place that smelled of—human living in a month. Of course I want to stay.

GITTEL. So stay!

(GITTEL *takes the hat out of his hand, drops it on the bed, gives him a towel, and disappears beyond the kitchen again. When* JERRY *opens the towel, it has a large hole in it. He shakes his head, amused, and rather forlorn.*)

JERRY. I feel ridiculous.

(*He walks out into the hall, leaving the door open. After a moment* GITTEL *comes back through the kitchen, still with her armful.*)

GITTEL. Listen, I— (*She sees the room is empty, stops, stares at his hat on the bed. She scowls at it, debating. Then she shakes her head, no, no, and walks back toward the kitchen with her armful. But on the threshold she halts. After a second she turns back, and stands to give the hat another stare. Finally she sighs, and with an air of disgusted resignation mutters to herself.*) Oh, what the hell, happy birthday.

(*And she puts everything back, her clothes back in the drawer, the clock back on the table, the pillow back in place alongside the other on the bed. She unbuttons and takes off her blouse, hangs it dangling on a chair, sits on the bed to remove her sandals, stands to slip her skirt off, walks in her half-slip and bra to a drawer again, takes out pajama-tops, and at this moment hears* JERRY *in the hall; she skedaddles with the pajama-tops into the darkness beyond the kitchen.* JERRY *returns, and walks around, restive. It is a moment before he accidentally kicks one of* GITTEL'S *sandals, stares at them, then at her skirt on the floor, then at her pillow next to his, and looking toward the kitchen, comprehends her intention. He takes up her blouse in his fingers. Bringing it to his face, he inhales the odor of woman again; he rubs it against his cheek, thinking, scowling. At last he comes out of the other end of some maze, and tells himself grittily:*)

JERRY. It's, not, a, *beginning.*

(*He hangs the blouse back on the chair, turns, picks up his hat from the bed, and walks straight out into the hall, closing the door behind him. After a moment* GITTEL *peers in from the kitchen, clad in the pajama-tops and carrying her underthings; she sees the room is still empty and comes in. Quickly she clicks off the* LAMP, *turns down the sheet, has her knee up to get in, remembers, and kneels around to the foot of the bed with her hand outstretched for* JERRY'S *hat. It is not there. She searches, baffled, then sees the door is now closed; she scrambles over the bed to it, looks along the hall to the john and then down over the bannister. Two stories down, there is the closing of the STREET DOOR. GITTEL comes back into her doorway, where she stands silhouetted; after a perplexed moment she slaps her thigh, in resignation.)*

### CURTAIN

## ACT ONE

### SCENE 3

*Both rooms.*

*It is several hours later, and the first light of DAWN is just beginning to pick out the furniture in both rooms. GITTEL is in her bed, asleep, with the blanket and sheet pulled up over her ears. JERRY'S room is empty, but after a moment we hear JERRY letting himself in at his door. When he opens it, he spies and bends to pick up a telegram waiting inside the threshold. He comes into his living room staring at it, unkempt, needing a shave, weary from walking all night, but relatively lighthearted. He takes the telegram to the broken window, tears the envelope open, then pauses in the act of lifting the message out, and presently shoves it back in, tosses it onto his couch, and lights a cigarette. He walks around a few steps, then stands deliberating between the telegram and the phone and suddenly sits to the phone. He dials, waits. The PHONE in GITTEL'S room rings. GITTEL rolls around before she is altogether awake, her hand fumbling till it finds the phone.*

GITTEL. (*Eyes closed.*) Yeah, h'lo. (JERRY *considers how to begin.*) H'lo!

JERRY. (*Dryly.*) About that ice-box. I think you let that other jerk have it too cheap.

GITTEL. Whah?

JERRY. If you keep handing things out to the first comer, judgment day will find you without an ice-box to your name, morally speaking.

GITTEL. (*Jerking up.*) Jerry! Hey, you all right? I called you two or three times, no answer.

JERRY. I tried another bridge. Queensboro, it opens a vast new territory to— (*He catches himself, breaks off.*) I was about to say get lost in, but that's my last hint. I walked out on you, Gittel.

GITTEL. Yeah. I noticed!

JERRY. What changed your iron-clad rule?

GITTEL. Oh—I couldn't resist your goddam hat!

JERRY. I should have left it for you. I thought it was something else.

GITTEL. Like what?

JERRY. Charity. I think your trouble is running the community chest.

GITTEL. Huh?

JERRY. My trouble is my wife does understand me. You lit a fair-sized birthday candle under me tonight, it cast a light backwards all the way to Omaha, Nevada.

GITTEL. How?

JERRY. Tess—her name is Tess, it comes back to me from time to time—also smothered me in loving kindnesses. But my God, if I hinted for them it's not all her fault. I needn't have gone into her father's law-office and I did, I needn't have let him set us up in a handsome house in Fairacres and I did, it poisoned the well.

GITTEL. (*Scowling.*) Well?

JERRY. Well. We had running water, but not much monogamy. I had to be heroic with some wife, no matter whose, and Tess now is marrying someone else, a colleague of mine who— (*He breaks this off.*) That's another chapter. I wanted to say only that tonight half my life looks like a handout, and I finally walked out on one. From you.

GITTEL. Oh. *I* thought it was something else.

JERRY. Such as?

GITTEL. I figured you figured I wasn't— (*She takes a*

*breath*.) I mean maybe you didn't think I was— You know.

JERRY. No.

GITTEL. Attractive!

JERRY. (*A pause.*) Oh, God. And you still called me two or three times?

GITTEL. (*She has her pride.*) *Two* times.

JERRY. Why?

GITTEL. Well, you disappear like that, I got worried about you.

JERRY. Gittel. (*His tone is gentle, very affectionate, for the first time genuinely heedful of her; the relationship is taking on a quite different color.*) Gittel, I'll tell you two truths. One, you're attractive, two, you don't look out for yourself.

GITTEL. Sure I do.

JERRY. No. If you did you'd object more.

GITTEL. What to?

JERRY. So many things. This minute, this very minute, why aren't you taking my head off about the time?

GITTEL. Why, what time is it?

JERRY. Little before five. It takes practice, go ahead.

GITTEL. Go ahead what?

JERRY. Practice. Protest. Enter an objection.

GITTEL. Huh?

JERRY. *Holler* at me!

GITTEL. What for?

JERRY. It's a hell of an hour to phone anyone. Who do I think I am, waking you up this time of night, my father-in-law? It shows no respect for you, you resent it, say so!

GITTEL. Look, what are you hollering at me for?

JERRY. (*Mildly.*) Your own good.

GITTEL. I don't like to holler at people, it makes me nervous. Anyway, I'm glad you phoned.

JERRY. Why?

GITTEL. (*Exasperated.*) What makes you so dumb? *I was worried about you!*

JERRY. That's better.

GITTEL. Better!

JERRY. All you need is practice. Go ahead.

GITTEL. (*Irately.*) Who's practicing? What do you think, I'm nuts, you know what time it is, is that what you call me up five o'clock in the morning to practice hollering?

JERRY. (*Amused.*) No, I called to say don't give anything else away. Until I see you.

GITTEL. What?

JERRY. I'm asking whether you'd—care to try being half of a pair?

GITTEL. (*A pause.*) Look, let's not go through all *that* again!

JERRY. On my terms, this time. And I don't mean as a handout.

GITTEL. So what do you mean?

JERRY. That *I'd*—like to look out for you. Hemorrhages notwithstanding. (GITTEL *stares at the phone.*) Will you let me?

GITTEL. (*Shakes her head, too uncertain about her feelings to know what to say; she is touched, and also wants to snicker.*) I'm—I—why?

JERRY. I think you can use me. Not that I'll be such a bargain, a lot of me is still tied up in the—civil wars. I thought I'd tell you the whole mess, if you'd have breakfast with me.

GITTEL. Where?

JERRY. Here. Will you come?

GITTEL. Well, I'm having a tooth pulled out eight-fifteen. I mean I'll be spitting a lot of goddam blood, we won't be able to *do* anything.

JERRY. Will you come?

GITTEL. Sure I'll come.

JERRY. (*A pause, gently.*) I'll look for you. (*He is about to hang up, when he has an after-thought.*) Gittel.

GITTEL. Yeah?

JERRY. What do you do when a tooth bleeds?

GITTEL. (*Concerned.*) Why, you got one?

JERRY. Oh, you're a character. I'm talking about *yours*.

GITTEL. Oh. Let it bleed, why? It dries up.

JERRY. I knew I'd have a use for that ice-box. I'll have a cake of ice in the sink.

GITTEL. What for?

JERRY. For the ice-bag I'll buy for your tooth.

GITTEL. (*A pause, amused.*) You're starting right in, huh?

JERRY. Not a minute to lose. It's a new day, in my thirty-fourth year, and I feel like a rising lark. Get some sleep, now.

(*He hangs up.* GITTEL *sits for a moment, then also hangs up and shakes her head in a kind of wonderment.*)

GITTEL. Sonofabitch.

(*Presently she gets up and goes into her kitchen, pours herself some milk from the pot, and comes back; she settles in bed with it.* JERRY *sets his phone on the floor and remains, smiling, until his eyes again encounter the telegram. He picks it up, fingers it. Finally he draws it out, takes it to the window, and reads it. He goes over it twice in silence; the third time he reads it aloud to himself, without expression.*)

JERRY. "I called to say happy birthday you stinker don't shut me out God help both of us but will you remember I love you I do Tess."

(*After a second he perceives the telegram is trembling. He crumples it in his hand, and drops it slowly out the broken window. He returns to his couch, transfers his clothes to the chair, and lies down to finish his cigarette. Each lies alone with his thoughts in the bleak light of daybreak;* JERRY *smoking and* GITTEL *sipping her milk; the only sound is some distant CHURCH CLOCK ringing five.*)

*END OF ACT ONE*

# ACT TWO

## SCENE 1

*Jerry's room.*

*It is October now, early evening, dusk. Gittel's room is much the same, with her bed unmade and two pillows rumpled; but a transformation has over-taken Jerry's. It has been fixed up inexpensively, and now is tidy, pleasant, livable, with bedspread, wall-lamp, throw-rugs, burlap drapes, stained fruit-crates for shelving—all improvements in the peasant style of Gittel's garb. Near the window there is a bridge-table with two chairs, set for dinner. Gittel's little RADIO is playing on a shelf, WNYC, sym-phonic music. The LIGHT in the kitchen is on, now agreeably shaded; out here GITTEL, wearing a dish-towel for an apron, is preparing dinner. She comes in carrying a bowlful of salad, sets it on the table, and stands listening thoughtfully to the music; she then has a kind of slow convulsion, which after a moment we see is a modern-dance movement, be-cause she stops, is dissatisfied, scratches her head, tries another, gives it up, and returns to the kitchen. Here she opens the gas-range cover to peer in, does some basting, closes it. In the middle of her next turn she halts, listens towards the door, then ske-daddles back in and hastily begins lighting two candles on the table. We then see JERRY opening the outer door.*

GITTEL. (*Calling happily.*) Hiya, baby.

JERRY. Hi. (*He stops, to sniff the oven, looks in.*) Hmm. Smells good, who's in here? Chicken!

GITTEL. And salad, and potatoes, and wine's on the ice.

JERRY. Wine, well. (*Coming into the doorway he leans there, just taking her in at the candles; he is in street-*

33

*clothes and hat, with a legal tome or two under his arm, and some parcels.*) What are we launching, me?

GITTEL. I got a bargain, sixty-nine cents a bottle. Must of been getting kind of old. (*She comes to kiss his amused face above her, and his arm draws her in.*) What's so funny?

JERRY. You are, infant. (*He spies the window over her shoulder.*) You put up curtains for me!

GITTEL. Sure, what do you think I come over for, just to see you?

JERRY. Very cozy. Last couple of weeks you've turned this into the showplace of the nation. You're better than wine, you improve with age.

GITTEL. What's in the bag?

JERRY. Everything's in the bag.

GITTEL. I mean this bag.

JERRY. Don't move!

GITTEL. (*Alarmed.*) Huh?

JERRY. Careful. Back in one inch.

GITTEL. Why?

JERRY. (*Soberly.*) Because all afternoon I've been totally surrounded by law-books, and I like it much better being totally surrounded by you. I got your thread. (*He jiggles a bag at her ear.*)

GITTEL. Oh, good. You see Frank Taubman, Jerry?

JERRY. I did. And dessert. (*He jiggles another bag.*) Soya cake. Salt-free, butter-free, flavor-free.

GITTEL. Well, what'd he say?

JERRY. You'll hear. And a piece of the moon. From me, to you. (*He deposits the third bag in her hand.*)

GITTEL. A present?

JERRY. Just a piece of the moon.

(GITTEL *unwraps it at the candles, while* JERRY *gets rid of his books and hat, takes off his jacket.*)

GITTEL. I can't wait to see what's in it, what's in it?

JERRY. (*Deadpan.*) Well, it turns out this way, she opens this box from her lover thinking it's candy but it's really the preserved brains of her unfaithful father, who has run away to join this gang of juvenile delinquents, she recognizes him instantly and lets out an unearthly shriek—

GITTEL. (*Blankly, lifts it.*) A cake of soap?

JERRY. (*Approaching.*) Supposed to be the preserved brains of—

GITTEL. What's the matter, I smell?

JERRY. Good idea, let's investigate. (*He puts his nose in her hair from behind, his arms around her waist.*)

GITTEL. I mean what kind of present is a cake of soap, I need a bath?

JERRY. What kind of present is a— Did you look at the box?

GITTEL. No.

JERRY. Read the soap.

GITTEL. (*By candlelight.*) Channel number—

JERRY. Channel number five, it's a TV sample. Chanel number five, girl, you're holding a two-fifty soap-bubble there.

GITTEL. (*Aghast.*) Two-fif—for *one* cake of soap?

JERRY. Don't you dare take a bath with that. We're going to eat it, spoonful by spoonful. Instead of that soya cake.

GITTEL. You know sometimes I think the nutty one of this twosome some of us think I am is you? Two-fifty, we won't eat!

JERRY. We'll eat, it will be a feast. How's your belly?

GITTEL. Oh fine. I took some banthine, it went away.

JERRY. Didn't all go away. Here's some.

GITTEL. Some what?

JERRY. Belly.

GITTEL. Oh. You think I'm too fat.

JERRY. Good God, no.

GITTEL. You think I'm too skinny?

JERRY. (*Dryly.*) I think you're a sacred vessel of womanhood.

GITTEL. Ahuh. Sexy as all get-out, that's why you buy me a hunk of soap.

JERRY. Buoyant in the bow, swively in the stern, and spicy in the hatch, how's that?

GITTEL. S'pretty good. (*They have been kissing; now* GITTEL *cocks her head back.*) You think I'm *too* sexy?

JERRY. Hm?

GITTEL. I mean oversexed?

JERRY. I think you're a mixed-up girl. Calmly considered, your bottom is tops.

GITTEL. Some vessel. Sounds like a shipwreck. (*She kisses him again. When they come up for air, she slides out of his hands.*) Anyway! You're getting a phone-call soon. Long distance.

JERRY. Who from?

GITTEL. (*Brightly.*) Your wife. (*She inhales at the soap again.*) This her kind, Jerry?

JERRY. (*A pause.*) No. And I seldom gave her gifts, she was—amply supplied.

GITTEL. Okay. (*She takes the soap out into the kitchen, busies herself at the oven.* JERRY *stands alone, not moving, for a long moment; then he calls out, sounding casual.*)

JERRY. When did she call?

GITTEL. (*Calling in.*) Soon's I got here. Said she'd call back eight o'clock. (JERRY *looks at his wristwatch, stares at the phone, clears the litter off the table, glances again at the phone, and goes to his window, to gaze out.* GITTEL *comes back in, bearing a casserole of chicken and a bowl- ful of French fries to the table, with cheerful chatter.*) She must have money to burn, huh? I mean *two* long- distant phone calls, ye gods. You know I only made one long-distant phone-call in my whole life? (*She stands serving out their portions.*) Tallahassee, that's in Florida, right after we were married. Wally had a job there. I mean he said he had a job, when I found out it was really a red-head he went back to I didn't drop dead either, but I called him up—

JERRY. I don't think I care to talk to her. (GITTEL *continues serving, but frowning over it.*) Gittel.

GITTEL. So don't. Anyway I got the bill, that's when I did drop dead.

JERRY. I won't answer.

GITTEL. (*Presently.*) All right. You want to get the wine?

JERRY. With pleasure. (*He turns the RADIO on, and goes into the kitchen.*) Let's drink life to the dregs, the whole sixty-nine cents worth. I have something for us to toast. I had a long session this afternoon with Frank— (GITTEL *meanwhile stares at the phone, then switches the RADIO off; the mood in the room changes, and the phone now begins to haunt what they do and say.* JERRY *returns with the wine and a corkscrew.*) What's the matter, honey?

GITTEL. I don't see any crowd.

JERRY. That I said I wouldn't answer?

GITTEL. Nothing's the matter!

JERRY. It's dead and buried. (*He uncorks the bottle.*) Six feet under, the coffin is sealed, the headstone is paid for, I'd rather not open it all up again. (*Lightly.*) Let's change the subject to something pleasant. How are you making out on your recital?

GITTEL. That's pleasant? I looked at that loft again— the goddam bastard still wants a two-year lease and won't come down a cent. I haven't got that kind of gelt. It's a very fine dance studio, for Rockefeller.

JERRY. You don't need Rockefeller, you have Fort Knox here.

GITTEL. Where?

JERRY. (*Taps his brow.*) I had a long session with Frank Taubman this afternoon.

GITTEL. So what'd he tell you? (*But her look is on the phone.*)

JERRY. That if I'm not a member of the New York Bar he could offer me only some briefs to prepare.

GITTEL. Oh.

JERRY. I'll go down with you in the morning and we'll give this goddam bastard two months rent.

GITTEL. Out of what?

JERRY. I accepted them. It pays per brief, we'll be papering the walls with gelt.

GITTEL. I'll get the loft when *I* get a job. (*Her look again is on the phone; this time* JERRY *notices.*)

JERRY. (*A pause.*) It didn't say anything.

GITTEL. Huh?

JERRY. The phone.

GITTEL. Yeah. I heard Schrafft's was putting on girls, I'm going to see about it tomorrow.

JERRY. Schrafft's. Waiting on table?

GITTEL. Whatever they got. I worked the candy counter for them last year, I put on seven pounds. It's very good candy.

JERRY. Do me a small favor, let me do you a small favor?

GITTEL. Sure. Like what?

JERRY. Like stake you to Loft's, instead of Schrafft's. You know how much I can earn doing briefs? A hundred a week, I'll *buy* you candy. It's absurd for you to work at Schrafft's.

GITTEL. What have you got against Schrafft's?

JERRY. I'm afraid someone there will eat *you* up. No Schrafft's, the prosecution rests. (*They eat again.*) You know this chicken is fabulous? What makes it taste like gin?

GITTEL. Gin.

JERRY. Fabulous. You can sew, you can cook, you— (*He suddenly takes note, ominously.*) What are we doing eating French fries?

GITTEL. You like them.

JERRY. Not after you were up half the night with a bellyache.

GITTEL. (*Indignant.*) You said they were your favorite.

JERRY. (*Mildly.*) My favorite will put holes in *your* stomach lining. And your stomach lining is my favorite, how many did you eat?

GITTEL. Three.

JERRY. (*Rises.*) Three too many.

GITTEL. I love them.

JERRY. (*Hesitates.*) Four is all you get. (*He lifts the potatoes from her plate in his fingers, drops one back and takes the bowlful out into the kitchen.*)

GITTEL. Hey! (*But the protest is weak, she contents herself with snaring others from* JERRY'S *plate in his absence, and pops them into her mouth. He comes back with a slice or two of bread.*)

JERRY. Here. Instead. You need starch to soak up the acids, honey, I've been reading up on the whole pathology of ulcers and you simply don't know what to do with your acids. In medical parlance we call this a half-acid diagnosis. Let's stick to what *you* can eat, hm?

GITTEL. (*Her mouth full.*) Certainly! (*JERRY about to sit consults his wristwatch, frowns, glances at the phone; then, sitting, finds* GITTEL'S *eyes on him.*) It didn't say anything!

JERRY. What?

GITTEL. The phone.

JERRY. Not going to, either. I was just thinking I'd forgotten the sound of her voice. How did she sound?

GITTEL. (*Scowling.*) What do you mean how did she sound?

JERRY. (*Bored.*) Only how did she sound, don't—

GITTEL. Lovely, she sounded lovely! You want to hear how she sounds, talk to her. What are you scared of?

JERRY. (*Puts down his fork, and contemplates her. Evenly.*) You really want me to answer it, don't you?

GITTEL. Who, me?

JERRY. Why?

GITTEL. Why not?

JERRY. Because I'm in a state of grace here in a garden of Eden with you and a stuffed chicken. Adam and Eve, and you know what that twelve hundred miles of phone cable is? The snake. Why let it in, it was enough work getting rid of the bedbugs.

GITTEL. Why do you hate her so?

JERRY. I don't, let's change the subject. (*They eat again.*) I'll go with you about this loft tomorrow. Tell the man I'm your lawyer, I handle nothing but your leases, I'll negotiate the whole transaction. I'll even bring my brief-case.

GITTEL. What kind of bread is this?

JERRY. Health bread. For our health.

GITTEL. Gee, they must cut this right off a *stump*, huh?

JERRY. (*Sits back and enjoys her.*) You're a bug. A waterbug, this way, that, what did I do to have you in my bloodstream? Look. I'm saying if you're a dancer it's time to do something about it, the days are going—

GITTEL. (*Vehemently.*) Of course I'm a dancer, it's driving me crazy! Everybody else is getting famous, all I'm getting is repair bills from Singer's!

JERRY. All right then, I can lend a hand with the loft. You go to work on the recital, I go to work on the briefs.

GITTEL. What's doing briefs?

JERRY. Researching a case for precedents. (GITTEL *is uncomprehending, so he clarifies it.*) When one cuke brings suit against another cuke, the court can't decide which cuke is cukier until it hears how two other cukes made out in *another* court in 1888.

GITTEL. So is that fun?

JERRY. Not unless you have a nose-in-the-book talent. But I won't be writing briefs for the rest of my life, I can practice in court here any time I take the state Bar exam.

GITTEL. So whyn't you take it?

JERRY. (*Smiles.*) It makes me nervous.

GITTEL. Aah. You'd knock them dead.

JERRY. What makes you think so?

GITTEL. (*Serenely.*) I got my impressions.

JERRY. I barely know the traffic laws here. Statutory law *varies*, from state to state, I—

GITTEL. So what, you could study up.

JERRY. (*Dryly.*) I'm a little old to go back to school.

GITTEL. Every day you read in the paper, some grandma going to NYU, eleven grandchildren, seventy years—

JERRY. Do I look like somebody's grandma? I'm not

*that* old, but I've been a practicing— (*But he breaks off and leans back to regard her for a moment. Then:*) How do you do it?

GITTEL. What?

JERRY. We begin with my saying I'll lend a hand, and end one minute later with you putting me through college.

GITTEL. I don't need a hand, I'll make out! (JERRY *is displeased with this, and after a moment lowers his face to his plate.*) You got to take the exam sometime, no?

JERRY. No.

GITTEL. So what'll you be here in your old age?

JERRY. Don't rush me into the grave. I'm not living that far ahead.

(GITTEL *is displeased with this, and after a moment lowers her face to her plate. They eat.* GITTEL *then bounces up, marches into the kitchen, returns with the bowl of potatoes, and drops a fistful into her plate.*)

GITTEL. What are you, on vacation here?

(*She sits.* JERRY *reaches over, puts the fistful back into the bowl, rises, and carries it out again to the kitchen. He returns without it.*)

JERRY. Not necessarily, but I *might* die somewhere else. Be a shame to go to all the trouble of taking the Bar exam in New York and die in New Jersey. I'd have to commute. (*He sits.* GITTEL *rises, and marches toward the kitchen again; but* JERRY *catches her wrist, pulls her onto his lap.*) Look, look. (*He reaches a long arm out to the couch, catches up one of the legal tomes, and deposits it open on* GITTEL's *thighs. She scowls at the text.*)

GITTEL. What?

JERRY. This is Clevenger. Civil Practice Act of New York, what I don't know fills this little volume and a library full besides. To take the Bar exam here. For two days in this state they lift open the top of your skull and stare in. Now—

GITTEL. Jerry, you know what I think you got too much of? Lack of confidence!

JERRY. Oh, great.

GITTEL. I mean ye gods, you were such a popular lawyer in Nevada, what's the difference?

JERRY. Nebraska, dear. (*He kisses her neck.*)

GITTEL. Nebraska, so what's the difference?

JERRY. About a thousand miles. You know you have a two-fifty smell without that damned soap?

GITTEL. (*Squirms.*) Giving me goose-pimples. Jerry, now I'm talking seri— (JERRY *turns her face, kisses her; after a moment she comes up for breath.*)—ous, how come you were so popular there if—

JERRY. (*Kissing her throat.*) I shot in the mid seventies.

GITTEL. (*Stares.*) Shot what?

JERRY. (*Kissing her chin.*) Birdies.

GITTEL. That made you *popular?*

JERRY. In the butterfly set. (*He kisses her mouth; this time she comes up with her eyes closed, takes a breath, and gives up.*)

GITTEL. Oh, damn you. (*She seizes his ears and kisses him fiercely; Clevenger slides to the floor, unnoticed, and the kiss goes on. Now the PHONE rings.* GITTEL's *head comes up. After a second* JERRY *draws it down with his hand, but the next ring brings her up scowling at it.*) Phone's ringing.

JERRY. (*Lightly.*) I don't want the world in. (*He draws her to him again; it rings again.*)

GITTEL. I can't!

JERRY. (*Puts her aside on her feet, gets up, crosses, takes the phone off the hook, drops it to hang and comes back.*) Better?

GITTEL. Oh, for Christ sakes. (*She ducks past him, and picks up the phone, combative.*) Yeah, hello—

JERRY. (*Outraged.*) Put down that phone!

GITTEL. So whyn't you call sooner— (JERRY *coming*

*swiftly snatches the phone from her, ready to slam it
down.*) It's *Larry!* (JERRY *stares at her, lifts the phone
to his ear, listens, then hands it to her, and walks away.*)
Hello? . . . No, we thought it was the—landlord. So
what's the Y say? . . . *How much?* (JERRY *stands staring out the window, which is now dark with night;*
GITTEL'S *eyes are on him.*) Well, listen, I can't— . . .
No, maybe we'll try Henry Street, but I can't think
about it now . . . I'm in the middle of eating, Larry,
I'll call you back later. . . . No, I can't swing the loft
yet, but I can't go into all that now.

(*She hangs up, and stands over the phone.* JERRY *leaves
the window; at the table he drains his tumbler of
wine in one swallow, sets it down. They stand silent
for a moment,* GITTEL *not taking her eyes from
him.*)

JERRY. (*Curtly.*) I'm sorry I shouted.

GITTEL. What did that bitch do to you?

JERRY. (*Rounding.*) Bitch? (*Grimly, then.*) Married
me, helped put me through law school, stood by me in
pinches. Loved me, if anyone did or could. She was never
a bitch, don't call her that again.

GITTEL. (*Nettled.*) That's why you left Nebraska, she
was so nice?

JERRY. I left because I couldn't take being in the same
town with her and her fiancé.

GITTEL. So you ran away.

JERRY. If that's what you call starting over from bed-
rock, yes, I ran away.

GITTEL. So stop running, it's the Atlantic Ocean
already.

JERRY. No one's running now.

GITTEL. You're running, why can't you talk to her on
the phone?

JERRY. (*Turns to look at her.*) Ask it of me. Don't do
it for me, ask it of me, perhaps I'll do it for you. Do
you want me to?

GITTEL. She's your wife.

JERRY. Do you want me to?

GITTEL. It's your phone.

JERRY. Do *you* want me to? Yes or no!

GITTEL. No!

JERRY. (*A pause.*) You want me to work here for Frank Taubman?

GITTEL. No.

JERRY. What *do* you want from me?

GITTEL. Not a goddam thing.

(*She lights a cigarette, takes a drag.* JERRY *passing removes it from her lips, and* GITTEL, *very annoyed, shakes another from his pack while he is stubbing the first out.*)

JERRY. Why do you smoke, you know it's not good for your stomach.

GITTEL. I'll keep track of my own stomach, we been together almost thirty years now, we get by!

(*She strikes the match to the new cigarette and* JERRY *turns. He observes her, not moving a muscle, until it comes in an outburst.*)

JERRY. Don't be such a damfool tower of strength!

GITTEL. What!

JERRY. I'm sick of it too, idiotic act of taking care of you and your weak stomach. Weak, you're as tough as wire.

GITTEL. So one of us better be!

JERRY. (*Stares at her grimly; when he speaks now it is level, but unsparing.*) And one of us better not be. You don't get by, you only tell yourself lies. From day to day, sure, job to job, man to man, you get by. And nothing sticks, they take off to Tallahassee. Did you pay his train fare? (*This is a mock question, but* GITTEL's *open mouth is a real answer.*) My God, you did! You pay the freight, and every bum climbs on for a free ride. And you never know why the ride is over, do you? I'll tell you why, when a man offers you a hand up you put a donation into it. Why don't you spit in it? So they use you and walk out. How many of them have you slept with on their way through, twenty-five? (*He waits.*) Fifty? (GITTEL *only stares, now he is inexorable.*) Five hundred? It's not a lark any more, you're not a kid, you're on the edge of a nightmare, and you're all alone. Who cares, but me? Don't spit in my hand, Gittel, whether you know it or not you need it. And make one claim, one real claim on a man, he just might surprise you. (*He waits:* GITTEL *continues to stare, palely, not answering.* JERRY'S *voice is hard:*) Do you get my point?

GITTEL. (*Shaken.*) Sure. (*Then she reacts, leap-frogging over her own feelings:*) You're a *terrific* lawyer, what are you bashful about?

JERRY. You didn't understand one word I—

GITTEL. Sure I did, and if I was the jury I'd send me up for five years, no kidding. (*She rises, escaping toward the kitchen;* JERRY *catches her wrists.*)

JERRY. *I'm* not kidding!

GITTEL. So what do you want? Let go my—

JERRY. Need someone!

GITTEL. Let me go, Jerry, you're hurting—

JERRY. Need someone!

GITTEL. For what? Let go my arms or I'll yell!

JERRY. You won't yell. Now you—

GITTEL. *Help!*

(JERRY *drops her wrists. She stumbles away from him, tears of pain in her eyes, and inspects her wrists.*)

JERRY. You little lunatic, someone will come.

GITTEL. Nobody'll come, it's New York. (*But her voice is trembling as she shows her arm.*) Look, I'm going to be all black and blue, you big ape! I ought to get out of here before you slug me.

JERRY. Slug you. Is that something you've learned to expect from your romances?

GITTEL. I expect the worst! When it comes to men I

expect the worst! (*Now she is struggling against the tears.*) Whyn't you pick up the phone if you're so goddam strong?

JERRY. Do you want me to?

GITTEL. I don't know where I stand here, it's a big question mark, why should *I* stick my neck out?

JERRY. (*Inexorably.*) Do you want me to?

GITTEL. I *will* get a job too, what's such a crime, just—cause I—won't— (*And finally the tears come; helpless with sobs she turns away, trying to keep her weeping as private as she can, and failing.*)

JERRY. (*Moved.*) Gittel, I—shouldn't have said all that—

GITTEL. (*Wheeling on him.*) All right, all right, I can scream my head off here and nobody comes, who can I count on besides me?

JERRY. Me, Gittel.

(*The PHONE rings. JERRY alone turns his eyes to it; he stands unmoving. GITTEL gets her sobbing in hand, and waits on his decision. It rings again, and at last she speaks.*)

GITTEL. You. Lean on you I'll fall in a big hole in Nevada somewhere.

(*She comes to the table to crush the cigarette, but JERRY stops her hand; he takes the cigarette from her, goes with it to the phone, and lifts the receiver.*)

JERRY. Yes? . . . Yes, speaking . . . (*A pause, while the connection is made; GITTEL stands, and JERRY takes a much-needed drag. His head comes up with the voice at the other end.*) Hello, Tess . . . (*His own voice starts out deliberately casual.*) No, I didn't care to talk to you the other times, I'm doing it now by special request. . . . What's that, woman's intuition? . . . Yes, she is. . . . (*GITTEL now moves to clear the dishes from the table, very quietly; she takes a stack out to the kitchen.*) Her name's Gittel. . . . I do, very much. . . . I didn't plan

to be celibate the rest of my days, wouldn't do you any
good. . . . And a year of it in your house didn't do me
any good. . . . (*Sardonically.*) Oh, I'll be glad to
represent you in the divorce. If your father will represent
me, I need a good lawyer to help take him to the clean-
ers. . . . (*Now more irritable:*) Oh, tell him to stuff it
up his—safe-deposit box, if I need money I can earn it.
. . . I have a job, I accepted one today. A girl, an apartment, a job adds up to a life, I'm beginning. . . . I have
no intention of contesting the divorce, tell Lucian he can
file any time, I'll enter a voluntary appearance. The
sooner the better. . . . I'm not interested in being *friends*
with you and your fiancé, you'll have to put up with each
other. . . . (*Now through his teeth:*) Tess, you can't
sink a knife in me and hope to leave a tender afterglow.
. . . (*Watching him with the cigarette we see what this
conversation is coming to cost him; he controls himself.
Now weary:*) Tess, are you calling me halfway across the
continent to talk about the furniture? . . . If the house
is haunted burn it, we'll split the insurance. . . . (GIT-
TEL *comes back in to clear what remains on the table.
Now shakily:*) I'm not unfeeling, *I* don't want to be
haunted either, my God, you made a choice, *get your
hand out of my bowels!* . . . (GITTEL *stiffens at this.*
JERRY *closes his eyes in pain.*) Tess . . . Don't . . .
Please—plea— (*The connection is broken.* JERRY *looks
at the phone, and slowly replaces it; he is drenched in
sweat, and sudden tears confuse his eyes; when he lifts
his hand for a prolonged drag, the cigarette is shaking.
He does not look at* GITTEL. *She reaches with her fingers
and pinches out each of the candles; the room goes dark
except for the light from the kitchen.* GITTEL *without a
word lies face down on the couch, and does not stir.*)
Gittel. (GITTEL *is silent.* JERRY *comes to stand above her,
puts a hand on her hair; she huddles away.*) Gittel, I—

GITTEL. (*Suddenly.*) It's not what you think!

JERRY. What isn't?

GITTEL. Larry says the Y wants six hundred and
twenty-five bucks for one night, that's where we been

saying we'd give it. I can't even get up sixty-five a month for a lousy loft! (*Another silence.*)

JERRY. (*Shakily.*) No. Let's look at the snake. (*He tugs the string to the overhead bulb, and its naked LIGHT floods the room. He stands, unsteady.*) Gittel. Turn around. Please. (*She lies unmoving.*) *Look at me!* (*She rolls half around now, to face him with her eyes smouldering.*) Don't pretend. It hurts, let me see it hurts—

GITTEL. What, what?

JERRY. How I can—drown in that well. I need you.

GITTEL. For what?

JERRY. Give me something to hold onto! How do I climb out, where do I get a—foothold here, who do I work *for,* what do I build on? I'm in limbo here and I'm —shaking inside. Gittel. Need *me* for something, if it's only a lousy loft.

GITTEL. (*Keeps her eyes on him for a long moment; then she comes through in kind, almost inaudibly.*) Sure it hurts. I'll never hear you tell me that.

JERRY. What?

GITTEL. That I got a—hand inside you.

JERRY. (*A pause.*) Meet me halfway.

GITTEL. (*Presently she smiles, wryly.*) You mean we look at that loft, huh? Okay. Now put out that goddam light, will you? (JERRY *tugs it out.*) C'mere, you— French fry potato. (*He comes, she clasps him around the neck, and pulls him down upon her; and they lie in the haven, rack, forcing-bed of each other's arms.*)

## CURTAIN


## ACT TWO

### SCENE 2

*Both rooms.*

*It is several weeks later, noon, a cold December day. In both rooms the heat is now on—in Gittel's from a gas-heater affixed to the wall, in Jerry's from a new*

*kerosene stove in the center of the floor. Gittel's
room is empty, the door ajar.* JERRY *is in his room,
lying in a spread of legs and legal papers on the
couch, with the telephone receiver tucked at his
shoulder, in the middle of a conversation.*

JERRY. . . . Yes. . . . Well, that was the issue in
McCuller v. Iowa Transfer, if a claimant not the con-
signee enters— . . . That's right, they appealed and it
was reserved. This outfit doesn't stand a Chinaman's
chance of collecting out there, Mr. Taubman, I don't—
. . . Hm? . . . All right: Frank. I don't think we
should even consider a settlement. . . . It's not going
out on a limb. Though many a lawyer would have a
fresh view of things from the end of a limb, I— . . .
Why, thank you. . . . No, the surprise is finding myself such an expert here on midwest jurispudence. . . .
I see what it proves, it proves an expert is a damn fool
a long way from home. . . . (*The PHONE in* GITTEL's
*room rings.*) No, taking the Bar exam is something I
need about as badly as a brain operation, what for?
. . . Why should they admit me to the Bar on motion?
. . . I'm familiar with the procedure, you sponsor me
and I deliver a truckload of Nebraska affidavits. Maybe
I can get the affidavits, I'm doubtful about the truck.
. . . If it saves me taking the Bar exam why not, but
why should you sponsor— . . . Full-time. I see. . . .
How much would they pay me?—just to keep it sym-
bolic. . . . 6500 what, two-dollar bills? . . . Not enough.
Mr.—Frank. If I'm useful to have around full-time
I'm worth at least 7500, and to nail me down will take
eight, so we'd have to begin talking at nine. . . . (*Gittel's PHONE rings again.*) I might be very serious, I'm
interested in being nailed down. . . . But not to the
cross, by a Bar exam. If you'll sponsor me on motion
I'll certainly see what affidavits I can dig out of Omaha—

(GITTEL *meanwhile runs in from the hall, to answer her
phone; she is clad in a nondescript wrap, and we
see her countenance is adorned with a white mus-*

*tache-smear and goatee-dab of bleaching cream.
Her mood is listless.*)

GITTEL. Yeah, hello? . . . Oh, Sophie, hiya. . . .

JERRY. (*Glancing at wrist-watch.*) . . . Yes, I can
take a cab up. . . .

GITTEL. . . . Good thing you called, how long am I
supposed to leave this stuff on? I look like a goddam
Kentucky colonel here. . . .

JERRY. . . . No, I was going to bring this Wharton
brief in after lunch anyway. . . .

GITTEL. . . . It itches. . . .

JERRY. . . . All right, men's grill at the St. Regis,
quarter past. . . .

GITTEL. . . . What old friend? . . . Sam? . . .

JERRY. . . . Yes. See you. (*He clicks down, again
consults his watch, and dials.*)

GITTEL. . . , What'd you tell him I'm going steady
for? I mean how do *you* know I'm going steady if I don't
know? . . . So let *me* shoo them off. . . . I don't know
what I sound worried about, I sound worried? . . .

JERRY. (*Busy signal.*) Come on, Sophie, get off that
damned line. (*He hangs up, and without collecting his
things walks out of his flat.*)

GITTEL. . . . Well, my stomach's been giving me a
pain in the behind. . . . No, everything's peachy. . . .
Oh, she's going to marry someone else. . . . I don't
*know* how I get involved in such a mix-up, anyway it's
not such a mix-up. . . . No, Wally was different. . . .
Milton was different. . . . Which Max? . . . (*She lo-
cates her mug of milk, and takes a swallow.*) Look, did
anybody ever buy me a loft before? . . . Yeah, *he*
used to bring me a Mr. Goodbar, that one still owes me
seventy-two bucks I'll never see again. The fact is I'm a
born victim! Here I am, practically thirty years old, I'm
just finding it out. . . . (JERRY *returns with a fistful of
mail, among which is a feminine blue envelope; it stops
him. He discards the others, rips it open and reads it,
troubledly.*) So who's *against* going steady? . . . What

do you think, I'm crazy? Take him home to meet Momma he'll leave New York in a balloon. . . . You don't understand—he plays *golf,* for instance. I never knew anybody personally played golf. . . . Oh, what do *you* know. . . . He's got a lot on the ball! He busts his brains all day over these briefs he's doing, then he comes down the loft and sweeps up for me, what do you think of that? . . . Sure! I made twenty-two bucks on that loft this month, and Molly's got this kids' class she's going to move in this week. . . .

JERRY. (*Consults his watch again; he returns to the phone and dials, one digit.*) Operator, I want to call Omaha, Nebraska, Atlantic 5756. . . .

GITTEL. (*Dispirited.*) . . . Yeah, I been working on my recital. Well, trying to. . . .

JERRY. . . . Algonquin 4-6099. . . .

GITTEL. . . . It's hard to get started again after so long, you know? . . .

JERRY. . . . Call me back, please. (*He hangs up, then slowly lifts the letter to his nostrils, in a faraway nostalgia.*)

GITTEL. . . . Maybe I'll take up golf instead. . . . Sure he talks to her. . . . About the divorce, she won't get off the pot! . . . Sophie, I *told* him talk to her, he *has* to talk with her, what are you bending my ear about? . . . Sophie, you're getting me mad. . . . Cause you're pestering me! . . . So don't be such a friend, be an enemy and don't pester me!

(*She hangs up irately, and commences to dial again. Before she completes the round,* JERRY'S *PHONE rings; he answers it.*)

JERRY. Yes? . . . All right. . . .

GITTEL. (*Busy signal.*) Oh, nuts. (*She hangs up, gathers some clothes, and goes into her back room.*)

JERRY. . . . Hi, Ruth, is your boss in? . . . Tell him it's his son-in-law. The retiring one. . . . Thank you, Ruth, I miss you folks too. . . . Hello, Lucian, how are you, don't answer that question. . . . (*He moves the phone out from his ear.*) No, I have a job, thanks, in fact I'm applying for admission to the New York Bar on motion. . . . Sure, tell Tess. She thinks the only feet I can stand on are hers. . . . I'm calling about her. I have a letter from her here, it has a St. Joe postmark. What's she doing in St. Joe? . . . (*He moves the phone out from his ear.*) Well, it didn't walk down there and mail itself. I've had a call in to her since Wednesday, there's nobody in the house. When did you see her, Lucian? . . . Drives where for three days? . . . Just drives? . . . I wish you'd spend more time around her, you're better than nothing. . . . I mean your idea of solicitude is a loud voice, Lucian, just talking to you on the phone is like a workout with dumbells. . . . (*He moves the phone out from his ear.*) Money isn't enough. I have too much to say on that, though, sometime I'll call you collect. . . . She's not all right, I can smell it between the lines here. . . . What girl? . . . Of course I have a girl here, I told Tess so. . . . You mean it's since *then* she's so— . . . Devastated by what? . . . My God, Lucian, I waited for a year, a solid year, till I didn't have an ounce of self-respect left in me! One ounce, I packed with it. . . . Is that her word, abandoned? Tell me how I can abandon another man's bride, I'll come to the wedding. . . . Lucian, listen. Keep an eye on her, will you? That's all I called to say. . . . And give her my best. (GITTEL *comes out of her back room, dressed for the street.* JERRY *hangs up, collects his topcoat, hat, and brief-case, consults his watch, then hurries to dial.* GITTEL *picks up her phone, dials, and* JERRY *gets a busy signal.*) Oh, hell.

(*He hangs up, and hastens out of his flat. His PHONE now rings once, twice, while* GITTEL *in her room stares at her phone with mounting indignation. On the third ring* JERRY *comes running back in, and grabs up his phone just in time to hear* GITTEL *addressing hers:*)

GITTEL. Ye gods, you were just there!

JERRY. I'm here.

GITTEL. Oh, Jerry!

JERRY. I called twice. Hasn't Sophie got anything better to do than to talk to you?

GITTEL. No. I called *three* times, who you been yakking with?

JERRY. I was talking to Omaha.

GITTEL. What, *again?*

JERRY. (*After a pause.*) What does that mean? I had a peculiar letter from Tess, she—

GITTEL. You ask her about the divorce?

JERRY. No. It was Lucian, I didn't get to the divorce. Tess seems sunk, her father says she—

GITTEL. (*Hastily.*) Jerry, I'm on my way to the loft, I got to hurry, what are you calling me about?

JERRY. I thought you were calling me.

GITTEL. Who?

JERRY. Never mind. I called Lucian because I had to know what's going on out there, he says Tess has shut herself off from—

GITTEL. (*Interrupting.*) Jerry, I got to run, you give me a ring tomorrow.

JERRY. (*Staring.*) What about tonight?

GITTEL. It's Friday, after the loft I'm going to Momma's.

JERRY. What's special about Friday?

GITTEL. Gefilte fish, good-bye.

JERRY. (*Protesting.*) Hey, we had a dinner— (*But* GITTEL *hangs up.* JERRY *looks at the empty phone, his voice dying.*) —date.

(*After a moment he also hangs up.* GITTEL *backs away from her phone, while* JERRY *glances at his watch; each is reluctant to leave.* GITTEL *halts,* JERRY *hesitates over his phone, both are tempted to try again; but neither does. After a melancholy moment they turn and leave, in opposite directions.*)
*CURTAIN*

## ACT TWO

### SCENE 3

*Gittel's room.*

*It is February now, a Saturday night, late. Both rooms
are dark, and the GLOW of the city plays in the
snowy night outside the windows. For a moment
there is no movement in either room. Then there is
the sound of a KEY at Gittel's and the door swings
open. GITTEL is silhouetted in the doorway, alone and
motionless, resting against the jamb from brow to
pelvis; then she pushes away, and comes unsteadily
in. There is a sprinkling of snow on her hair and
overcoat. She lets her purse drop on the floor,
weaves her way around the bed without light except from the hall, and in the kitchen gets herself a
glass of water at the sink; she drinks it, fills another,
brings it in, and sits on the bed, with head bowed
in her hand. After a moment she reaches to click on
the LAMP, takes up her address-book, and searches
for a number. She dials it, and waits; when she
speaks her voice is tired and tipsy.*

GITTEL. Dr. Segen there? . . . *I'm* calling, who are
you? I mean are you really there or are you one of
these answering nuisances? . . . So can you reach Dr.
Segen for me? . . . Yeah, it's an emergency. . . . Gittel
Mosca, I used to be a patient of his, will you tell him
I'm very sick? . . . Canal 6-2098. . . . Thanks. *(She
gets rid of the phone, and still in her overcoat, drops
back onto the bed. The LAMPLIGHT is in her eyes,
and she puts up a fumbling hand to click it off. She lies
in the dark, an arm over her face. After a second JERRY
in top-coat and hat comes silently up, around the bannister in the hall, and into the doorway, where he stands.
The snow has accumulated thickly on him. He sees
GITTEL'S purse on the floor, picks it up, sees the key*

*still in the lock, and draws it out; it is this sound that brings* GITTEL *up on her elbow, startled, apprehensive.*) Oh! Hiya, Jerry. Where'd you blow in from? (JERRY *regards her, his manner is heavy and grim, and hers turns light.*) How was *your* party, have a good time?

JERRY. Not as good as you. Are you drunk, at least?

GITTEL. (*With a giggle.*) I had a couple, yeah. I had this terrible thirst all night, you know, I didn't stop to think. I mean think to stop.

JERRY. (*Drops the key in her purse, tosses it on the bed, and closes the door; he walks to the window, silent, where he leans against the casing, not removing his hat. Then.*) Let's get it over with, who was the wrestler?

GITTEL. What wrestler?

JERRY. The fat-necked one who brought you home just now.

GITTEL. Jake? (*She sits up.*) He's not a wrestler, he's a very modern painter.

JERRY. That's why you kiss him good night, you're a patroness of the arts?

GITTEL. (*Staring.*) Where were you?

JERRY. One jump behind you. In more ways than one.

GITTEL. I didn't kiss him, he kissed me. Didn't you go to Frank Taubman's party— (*She pushes herself to her feet, changes her mind, and sits again, shivering.*) Light the gas, will you, honey, I'm awful cold.

(JERRY *after a moment takes out matches, and kneels to the GAS-HEATER. When it comes on, it illuminates* GITTEL *drinking the glass of water in one gulp;* JERRY *rising sees her, and comes over to grip her wrist.*)

JERRY. You've drunk enough.

GITTEL. It's water! (JERRY *pries her fingers loose, and tastes it. He gives it back.* GITTEL *grins.*) What's the matter, you don't trust me?

JERRY. Trust you. You were in his cellar in Bleecker Street for an hour.

GITTEL. (*Staring.*) How do you know?

JERRY. What was he showing you, great paintings, great wrestling holds, what? (GITTEL *does not answer, and* JERRY *yanks on the LAMP, sits opposite her on the bed, and turns her face into the light.*) *What?*

(*She only reads his eyes and* JERRY *reads hers, a long moment in which she might almost cry on his shoulder, but she ends it with a rueful little snigger.*)

GITTEL. So what do you see, your fortune?

JERRY. Yours. And not one I want to see. You look trampled, is that what you're in training to be?

GITTEL. (*Irked.*) Ye gods, I had about six drinks, you think I'm ruined for life?

JERRY. I don't mean anything so wholesome as drink. You slept with him, didn't you?

GITTEL. Whyn't you take off your hat and stay awhile? (*She pushes his hat back from his eyes, then touches his temple and cheek.*) Poor Jerry, you—

JERRY. (*Puts her hand down.*) You slept with him.

GITTEL. You want to cry? I want to cry.

JERRY. (*Grimly.*) Differences aren't soluble in tears, this city would be one flat mudpie. *Did* you sleep with him?

GITTEL. (*But she rolls away into a pillow, her back to him.*) We both know I'm dumb, whyn't you talk plain words a normal dumb person could understand?

JERRY. How plain, one syllable?

GITTEL. Yeah.

JERRY. Fine. Did he lay you? (GITTEL *lies averted in silence, her eyes open.*) I asked did he—

GITTEL. So what if he did, that's the end of the world?

(*Now she does rise, to get away from him, though she is wobbly, and soon drops into a chair.* JERRY *puts his fingers to his eyes, and remains on the bed; it takes him time to come to terms with this.*)

JERRY. Maybe. Of this world. (*But he can't hold the anger in, he smacks the glass off the night-table and is on his feet, bewildered and savage, to confront her.*) Why? *Why?*

GITTEL. (*Wearily.*) What's it matter?

JERRY. It matters because I'm at a crossroads and which way I send my life packing turns on you! And so are you, you want to watch *your* life float down the sewer out to sea? You care so little?

GITTEL. I don't know, I—

JERRY. For me?

GITTEL. Oh, Jerry, I—

JERRY. For yourself?

GITTEL. Myself, I got other things to worry—

JERRY. Why did you *want* to?

GITTEL. I don't *know* why! Anyway who said I did?

JERRY. (*Glaring at her.*) You'll drive *me* to drink. *Did you or didn't you?*

GITTEL. Well, he may of slept with me, but I didn't sleep with him.

JERRY. (*Stares at her, tight-lipped for patience.*) All right, let's go back. Why did you go home with him?

GITTEL. It's a long story, I used to go with Jake two three years ago—

JERRY. Not that far back. Get to tonight.

GITTEL. So tonight I had a couple of drinks too many, I guess it was—just a case of old lang syne.

JERRY. Old lang syne—

GITTEL. *You* know.

JERRY. Yes, I'm an expert in it, especially tonight. Why did you drink?

GITTEL. (*Bored.*) You're supposed to be at the Taubman's having a good time.

JERRY. Is that why?

GITTEL. Nah, who wants to go there, for God's sake?

JERRY. I went about this trouble with the affidavits, I left as soon as I could to pick you up at Sophie's, you were just coming out with him giggling like a pony.

GITTEL. (*Indignantly.*) I was plastered, I said so, you want a *written* confession?

JERRY. You don't get plastered and flush us down the drain for no reason, and Taubman's party isn't it. I'm after the— (*She gets up wearily, again to move away from him.*) Don't walk away from me! I'm talking to you.

GITTEL. So go ahead, talk. Lawyers, boy.

JERRY. Because when something happens to me *twice* I like to know why. I'm after the reason, what did I do *this* time, what's your complaint?

GITTEL. Who's complaining? *You* are!

JERRY. My God, I have no right?

GITTEL. Don't get off the subject.

JERRY. It's the subject, I'm talking about you and me.

GITTEL. Well, I'm talking about your wife!

(*A silence.* GITTEL *walks, rubbing her stomach with the heel of her hand.* JERRY *quiets down, then.*)

JERRY. All right, let's talk about her. She's interested in you too, I feel like an intercom. What about her?

GITTEL. I saw your last month's phone bill. Omaha Neb 9.81, Omaha Neb 12.63—Whyn't you tell me you were the world's champion talkers?

JERRY. I like to keep in touch, Gittel, she's having a very rough time.

GITTEL. So who isn't? I got a headache, lemme alone.

JERRY. What's your case, I'm unfaithful to you with my wife over the phone, it's the phone bill pushes you into bed with this what's-his-name jerk?

GITTEL. Jake.

JERRY. Jerk! It could be you're pushing me into Grand Central for a ticket back, has that thought struck you? Is that what you want, to cut me loose? So you can try anything in pants in New York you've overlook— (*But* GITTEL *has flooped across the bed, face down, and lies still and miserable.* JERRY *contemplates her, his anger going, compassion coming, until he resigns himself with a sigh.*) All right. All right, it can wait till tomorrow. We'll battle it out when you're on your feet.

(*He drops his hat on a chair, comes over to the bed, kneels and begins untying her shoes. This kindness sends* GITTEL *off into a misery, her shoulders quiver, and she whimpers.*)

GITTEL. Oh, Jerry—

JERRY. What's the matter?

GITTEL. You don't like me any more.

JERRY. I hate you, isn't that passionate enough? Turn over. (GITTEL *turns over, and he starts to unbutton her overcoat; her hands come up, his ignore them.*)

GITTEL. I can do it.

JERRY. It's a huge favor, have the grace not to, hm?

GITTEL. (*Desisting.*) You don't hate me.

JERRY. I wouldn't say so.

GITTEL. You just feel sorry for me.

JERRY. What makes you think you're so pathetic? Pull.

GITTEL. (*Freeing one arm.*) Ever saw me dancing around that loft, boy, you'd think I was pathetic. I been sitting on that goddam floor so many hours I'm getting a callus, I wait for ideas to show up like I'm—*marooned* or something. So the dawn came, after all these years, you know what's wrong?

JERRY. (*Pausing, gently.*) You're not a dancer?

GITTEL. (*Staring.*) How'd you know?

JERRY. I didn't. I meant that loft as a help, not just to puncture a bubble.

GITTEL. So if I'm not a dancer, what am I?

JERRY. Is that why you got crocked? Turn over. (GITTEL *turns back over, and he slips the coat from her other arm and off; he begins to unbutton her blouse in back.*) Will you drink coffee if I make some?

GITTEL. (*Shuddering.*) No.

JERRY. Or an emetic? Get the stuff off your stomach?

GITTEL. You mean vomit?

JERRY. Yes.

GITTEL. (*Breaking away from his fingers in a sudden vexation, she rolls up to glare at his face.*) Why we always talking about my stomach? I got no other charms? (JERRY *reaches again.*) Get away! (*She pulls the still-buttoned blouse over her head, gets stuck, and struggles blindly.*)

JERRY. (*Compassionately.*) Gittel. (*His hands come again, but when she feels them she kicks out fiercely at him.*)

GITTEL (*Muffled.*) I don't want your goddam favors!

(*One of her kicks lands in his thigh, and stops him. GITTEL then yanks the blouse off with a rip, slings it anywhere, which happens to be at him, drags the coat over her head on her way down, and lies still. A silence.*)

JERRY. (*Then.*) I'm sorry you don't. I could use it. (*He retrieves the blouse, draws the sleeves right-side out, and hangs it over a chair, then stands regarding her.*) That's how you intend to sleep it off? (GITTEL *under the coat neither moves nor answers.*) Gittel? (*Again no answer.*) You want me to stay or go? (*After a wait* JERRY *walks to his hat, picks it up.*) Go. (*He looks at the gas-heater, pauses.*) Shall I leave the gas on? (*No response from under* GITTEL's *coat.*) Yes. You need me for anything? (*He waits.*) No. Of course not.

(*Presently he puts the LAMP out, walks around the bed to the door, and opens it. But he stands. Then he bangs it shut again, throws his hat back at the chair and walks in again after it.* GITTEL *then sits up to see the closed door, and gives a wail of abandonment.*)

GITTEL. Jerry—Jerry—

JERRY. (*Behind her.*) What?

GITTEL. (*Rolls around, to see him staring out the window. Indignant.*) What are you still here?

JERRY. I *can't* put it off till tomorrow.

(*He catches up a newspaper and rolls it in his hands as he paces, grimly.* GITTEL *kneels up on the bed and regards him.*)

GITTEL. What's ailing *you?*

JERRY. I have to talk. I called home today.

GITTEL. So what'd she say for herself this time?

JERRY. I didn't talk to her. (*He paces.*) I can't get the court affidavits I need there unless I ask her father to pull strings for me. I called to ask, and couldn't get my tongue in the old groove.

GITTEL. So hooray.

JERRY. Yes, hooray. It means the Appellate Division here won't admit me, on motion. I want my day in court. I've got to get out from behind that pile of books into a courtroom, and I'm at a dead end here. With one way out, the March Bar exam.

GITTEL. So take it.

JERRY. I'm *scared.* I've been under Lucian's wing all my professional life, I'm not sure myself what's in my skull besides his coattails, if I take that exam I'm putting everything I am in the scales. If I flunk it, what?

GITTEL. What else can you do?

JERRY. (*Slowly.*) I can live where I *am* a member of the Bar.

GITTEL. (*Stares at him, and neither moves; then she sits back on her heels. Unbelieving.*) You want to go back. (*The PHONE rings.* GITTEL *glances at it with sharp nervousness, knowing who it is, then back at* JERRY.) Go on.

JERRY. Answer it.

GITTEL. No. Go on. (*It rings again, and* JERRY *walks to it, the roll of newspaper in his hand.*) Let it ring! I won't talk to anybody.

(*Her alarmed vehemence stops* JERRY, *he stares at her.*

*The PHONE rings a few times throughout the following, then ceases.)*

JERRY. *(Sharply.)* Who is it, this late, him?

GITTEL. I don't know. So you going or not?

JERRY. *(Angered.)* Why not? I can make three times the money I earn here, to do the work I'm starved for, it tempts me and what's so tempting here, Jake? Beat my head against a Bar exam when I'm building here on what, Jake, kicks in the belly, quicksand?

*(GITTEL offers no answer. He turns back to the window. GITTEL now digs in her purse for a bottle of banthine tablets.)*

GITTEL. What do you think *I'm* up to my neck in here, not quicksand? *(She goes out into the kitchen, where she puts on the light and sets a pot of milk up to warm.)*

JERRY. *(Turns after her.)* All right, then tell me that! If something sticks in your throat you can't spit it out? It's so much *quicker* to hop in with the first gorilla you meet instead? How *dare* you treat yourself like a hand-me-down snotrag any bum can blow his nose in?

GITTEL. *(She is shaken by this; but she avoids him and comes back in, cool as metal, unscrewing her bottle of tablets.)* Okay. When?

JERRY. When what?

GITTEL. When you going?

JERRY. *(Heavily.)* Look. Don't rush *me* off to Tallahassee. I don't turn loose so easy.

GITTEL. Well, I got to make my plans.

JERRY. What plans, now?

GITTEL. *(Unconcernedly.)* I'll probably hook up with Jake again. He's got a lot to give a girl, if you know what I mean, you'd be surprised.

*(JERRY stands like a statue, GITTEL with a not unmalicious twinkle gazing back at him. Then his arm*

*leaps up with the roll of newspaper to crack her
across the side of the head, it knocks her off balance
and the bottle of tablets flies out of her hand in a
shower; she falls on the bed.*)

JERRY. (*Furious.*) That's not all I mean to you! *Now
tell the truth, once!* (GITTEL *holds her cheek, never taking her eyes from him.* JERRY *then looks around, stoops
and picks up the tablets and bottle, reads the label, sees
what it is. He goes into the kitchen. He pours her milk
into the mug, and brings it back in. He hands her the
mug, which* GITTEL *takes, still staring at his face while
he weighs the tablets in his palm.*) How many?

GITTEL. Two. (JERRY *gives her two, and she swallows
them with a mouthful of milk. He replaces the others in
the bottle.*)

JERRY. If your stomach's bothering you, why don't you
go to a doctor?

GITTEL. What do I want to go to the doctor? He tells
me don't have emotions.

JERRY. (*Screws the cap back on the bottle, tosses it on
the bed, and regards her.*) How bad is it?

GITTEL. It's not bad!

JERRY. Did I hurt you?

GITTEL. Sure you hurt me. What do you think my
head's made, out of tin? (*She waits.*) You didn't say
you're sorry.

JERRY. You had it coming. Didn't you?

GITTEL. Sure.

JERRY. I'm sorry.

GITTEL. (*Now takes a sip of milk, holding it in both
hands like a child; then she looks up at him with a grin.*)
You see? I said you'd slug me and you did.

JERRY. Makes you so happy I'll oblige every hour.

GITTEL. (*Ruefully.*) Who's happy? Boy, what a smack.
(*She explores her cheek, tentatively, with one palm.*)
Okay, so you're *not* going! (*She eyes him cheerfully, but*
JERRY *turns away from her.*)

JERRY. I didn't finish. (*He stands at the window, to*

*gaze down at the street.*) Now the divorce plea is in, Tess is in a—tailspin. Lucian thinks she won't remarry.

GITTEL. (*This is worse than being hit, and she can only sit and stare. At last.*) Oh, brother. You stand a chance?

JERRY. Maybe. (*But he shakes his head, suddenly wretched at the window:*) I don't know what or where I stand, what to put behind me, what's ahead, am I coming or going, so help me, I—

(*He breaks it off.* GITTEL *hugs her shoulders together, she is cold; it takes her a moment to find desperation enough to try to go over the edge.*)

GITTEL. All right, Jerry, I'll tell you the truth. I— (*She looks for where to begin.*) About tonight and Jake, I—did want to go to Frank Taubman's. Only I don't fit in with your classy friends. Like she would.

JERRY. (*Turns and looks at her.*) What?

GITTEL. What do you think, I don't know? (*She is hugging herself, shivering a little as she makes herself more naked, but trying to smile.*) I mean all I am is what I am. Like Wally, he wanted me to get braces on my teeth, I said so face it, I got a couple of buck teeth, what did I keep it, such a secret? I said you got to take me the way I am, I got these teeth.

JERRY. You're a beautiful girl. Don't you know that?

GITTEL. But I'm not her. And she's all you been thinking about since the minute we met.

JERRY. No.

GITTEL. Yes. So what's Jake, a—piece of penny candy. It's like when I was a kid, we used to neck in the vestibule, she's inside you and I'm always in the vestibule! You never gave me a chance. Okay, but then you say need you. I need you, I *need* you, who has to say everything in black and white? (*She rises to confront him, pressing the heel of her hand into her stomach.*) But if you want I should of just laid down and said jump on me, no, Jerry. No. Cause I knew all the time you had it in the back of your head to—prove something to her—

JERRY. To myself.

GITTEL. To her. Everything you gave me was to show her, you couldn't wait for a goddam *letter* to get to her. So when *you*—ask *me* to—hand myself over on a platter— (*She has endeavored to be dispassionate, but now it is welling up to a huge accusatory outcry:*) For what? For *what?* What'll I *get?* Jake, I pay a penny, get a penny candy, but you, you're a—big ten-buck box and all I'll get is the cellophane! *You short-change people, Jerry!* (JERRY *takes this indictment moveless, but rocked, staring at her.* GITTEL *hugs herself, tense, waiting till she has hold of herself.*) And that's the truth. That's what you did *this* time.

(*A silence. She waits upon him, intent, still tense, so much hangs on this; while he absorbs it painfully in his entire anatomy.*)

JERRY. (*Then.*) You mean I want a—complete surrender. And don't give one.

GITTEL. Yeah. Is that all I said?

JERRY. (*Closes his eyes on her.*) This time. And last time too. Because I short-changed her also, didn't I?

GITTEL. (*Desperate.*) I'm not talking about *her* now, that's exactly what I'm talking about!

(*But it takes* JERRY *unhearing away from her to the bureau, averted.* GITTEL *gives up, sits, slaps her chair, and puts her head in her hands.*)

JERRY. It's true. God help me, it's true, half of me isn't in this town.

GITTEL. So I tried Jake.

JERRY. Of course.

GITTEL. Okay, a snotrag. So we're both flops.

JERRY. Both? (*And presently he nods. But when he turns his gaze to her, and takes in her forlorn figure, his eyes moisten.*) No. Not altogether. (*He comes to stand behind her; she does not lift her head.*) All these months I've been telling you one thing, infant, you live wrong. I wanted to make you over. Now I'll tell you the other thing, how you live right. (*He gazes down at her hair, moves his hand to touch it, refrains.*) You're a gift. Not a flop, a gift. Out of the blue. God knows there aren't many like you, so when he makes one it's for many poor buggers. Me among many. (*He shakes his head, slowly.*) The men don't matter. I promise you, *the men don't matter.* If they use you and walk out, they walk out with something of you, in them, that helps. Forget them, not one of them has dirtied you. Not one has possessed you, nobody's even gotten close. I said a beautiful girl, I didn't mean skin deep, there you're a delight. Anyone can see. And underneath is a street-brawler. That some can see. But under the street-brawler is something as fresh and crazy and timid as a colt, and virginal. No one's been there, not even me. And why you lock them out is—not my business. (*He finds his hat, stands with it, not looking at her now.*) What you've given me is— something I can make out with, from here on. And more. More. But what I've given you has been—What? A gift of *me*, but half of it's a fraud, and it puts you in bed with bums. That colt needs an unstinting hand, infant. Not Jake, not me. (*He walks to the door, opens it, pauses, looking for a final word, and gives it across his shoulder.*) I love your buck teeth.

(*After a moment he starts out, and* GITTEL's *head comes up.* JERRY *is on the stairs when she stumbles around her chair, and cries out the doorway after him.*)

GITTEL. Jerry! Don't go! (JERRY *halts, not turning.*) The main thing *I* did in Jake's was—faint in the john. That's when I found I— (*Her voice breaks, the tremor in it is out as a sob.*) I'm bleeding, Jerry!

JERRY. (*Wheels on the stairs.*) What!

GITTEL. It's why I was so thirsty, I'm—scared, Jerry, this time I'm scared to be bleeding—

JERRY. Gittel! (*He runs back in, to grip her up by the arms; she leans on him.*)

GITTEL. Help me, Jerry!

JERRY. (*Stricken.*) Who's your doctor?

GITTEL. It's all right, you just got to get me to the hospital—

JERRY. *Who's your doctor?*

GITTEL. Segen. In my book, it was him calling, I didn't want you to know—

JERRY. You *lunatic.* Lie down, you—crazy, crazy—nitwit— (*He turns her to the bed, where she lies down; JERRY sits with her, and looks for the number in her book.*)

GITTEL. (*Weeping.*) Jerry, don't hate my guts.

JERRY. Why didn't you *tell* me?

GITTEL. I didn't want to trap you—trap you in anything you—

JERRY. Trap me? *Trap* me?

GITTEL. I hate my goddam guts, I'm so ashamed, but don't leave—

JERRY. Oh God, shut up, you—lunatic girl—

GITTEL. Don't leave me, don't leave me—

JERRY. I'm not leaving! (*He finds the number, bends to her face on his knee.*) I'm *here,* infant. Take it easy, can't you see I'm here? (*He kisses her; then he commences to dial with his free hand,* GITTEL *pressing the other to her cheek.*)

### END OF ACT TWO

# ACT THREE

## Scene 1

*Gittel's room.*

*It is March now, midday, sunny and warm. Jerry's room has an unused look—the window is closed and the shade pulled down, a pillow in its bare ticking lies on the couch, the curtain drawn back on the clothes-closet corner reveals chiefly empty hangers. In Gittel's room the window is open and the SUNLIGHT streams in. The furniture has been rearranged. Jerry's suitcase is in a corner. The sewing-machine and dress-dummy are gone, and in their place is a table littered with law-books, mimeographed sheets and syllabuses, notebooks, pencils in a jar, a desk-lamp, Jerry's portable typewriter, a coffee-cup, a dirty plate or two, a saucer full of butts. The night-table by Gittel's bed has become a medicine-table, studded with bottles and glasses, including one of milk; a new and more expensive RADIO is also on it, playing softly. GITTEL herself in a cotton night-gown is in the bed, pale, thin, and glum. She lies with her head turned to gaze out the window. The hefty book she has been trying to read rests on her lap, her finger in it, and she is not hearing the radio, until the MUSIC stops and the ANNOUNCER begins, cheerfully. What he has to say is that this is WQXR, the radio station of the New York Times, to be fully informed read the New York Times, and wouldn't she like to have the New York Times delivered every morning before breakfast so she could enjoy its world-wide coverage while sipping her coffee, join the really smart people who—*

GITTEL. (*Disgusted.*) Aah, shut up, what do you know.

(*She dials him out, and gets some MUSIC elsewhere; but she is in no mood to listen, and clicks it off altogether. She then opens the book again, and scowls with an effort of concentration over the page. But she heaves a gloomy sigh, and the book immediately afterwards: it hits the floor and almost hits a flinching* JERRY, *who is opening the door with his foot, his arms laden with law-books and groceries, his topcoat over his shoulder, his hat back on his head.* GITTEL *brightens at once.*)

JERRY. Hold your fire, I'm unarmed!

GITTEL. Jerry, honey, I thought you'd never be home.

JERRY. (*Bends to kiss her, then drops his law-books and coat and a gift box on the table. Throughout the scene he attends to a variety of chores in an unpausing flow, without leisure really to stop once; he is in something of a fever of good spirits. He indicates the gift box.*) I came home a roundabout way, to bring you something from China. Though they met me more than halfway.

GITTEL. You don't have to bring presents.

JERRY. After lunch. I got in a tangle with old Kruger on this Lever contract, I have to be back by one. (*He bears the groceries out to the kitchen.*)

GITTEL. (*Darkly.*) That's two minutes ago.

JERRY. Yes, if I hurry I'll be late. I had a great morning though, I bore down on the old barracuda and he only opened his mouth like a goldfish. All those barracudas seem to be shrinking, lately, must be the humidity. What kind of morning you have?

GITTEL. So so.

JERRY. (*Not approving.*) Just lay here?

GITTEL. I almost got up to go to the john.

JERRY. Ah, that will be the day, won't it?

GITTEL. Yeah. Be in all the newsreels. (JERRY *in silence in the kitchen lights the oven, unwraps a small steak, slides it under the broiler.*) I'll try for the john tomorrow, Jerry, I'm pretty wobbly.

JERRY. What do you expect the first time, to climb Mount Everest?

GITTEL. (*A pause.*) *That's* what they go up there for? (*She gazes out the open window, while* JERRY *opens a can of potatoes, and dumps them in a pot to warm.*) You know where I'd like to be this minute?

JERRY. In bed, or you'd be out of it.

GITTEL. Central Park. On the grass. I don't get any *use* out of Central Park, you know? Specially a day like this, I mean here spring isn't even here and spring is here.

JERRY. (*Comes back in, unknotting his tie, en route to the bureau to rummage in its drawers.*) I'll make you a proposition, will you shoot for the stairs by Friday afternoon?

GITTEL. (*Uneasily.*) Why?

JERRY. I called Dr. Segen again this morning, he emphatically recommended a change of venue. I'll take you to Central Park in a cab Friday afternoon, is it a date?

GITTEL. What's Friday afternoon?

JERRY. The exam's over, I'd like to collapse in Central Park myself. Be down to get you in a taxi, honey, straight from the Bar exam. Date?

GITTEL. (*Evading it.*) One thing I'll be glad when that exam's over, maybe you'll stop running long enough to say hello.

JERRY. (*Obliges, with a smile.*) Hello. Date?

GITTEL. (*Scowling.*) I just sit on the edge here, I feel like my stomach's a—cracked egg or something. I don't want any more leaks.

JERRY. (*Gives her a severe eye while he hangs his jacket over a chair and takes a batch of mail out of its pocket.*) Doctor says if you don't get out of bed this week all your blood will rust. I really couldn't afford that hello, I didn't have a minute yet to look into who's writing me what here. (*He hurries through the envelopes, discarding them one by one onto the bed.*) Harper's wants me to buy their complete works, haven't time to read why. Hospital bill, ouch. Smoke it after dinner, on the gas stove. Clerk of the District Court, Omaha— (*But this one stops him short. He carries it away from her, rips it open, unfolds a legal document, in blue backing distinctive enough to be remembered later, and stares at it.*)

GITTEL. Anything?

JERRY. (*A silence.*) Legal stuff. Coming out of my ears these days, I— (*He finds it difficult to lift his eyes from it, it takes him an effort, but he drops document and envelope on the table and gets back into stride.*) Here, before I forget. (*From his jacket he brings a check out and over to* GITTEL.) I let Molly's class in the loft, she gave me a check for you. She'll leave the key over the door, I'll pick it up before cram-school.

GITTEL. Gee, Jerry, you shouldn't take time. (*She takes his hand as well as the check, and puts her cheek to it.*) You're okay.

JERRY. It's your money I'm after, infant.

GITTEL. (*Brightly.*) Yeah, it pays to be a big fat capitalist, huh? Lay here, it just rolls in.

JERRY. (*Stooping.*) And this rolls out. Get up today or forever hold your peas. (*He comes up with a bedpan from under the bed, and bears it into the back room, while* GITTEL *stares.*)

GITTEL. Hey, what's the— My God, I lost a quart of blood!

JERRY. I bought you three pints, that's a handsome enough profit. Capitalists who aren't satisfied with fifty per cent end up in the federal hoosegow. (*On his way back he picks up the book and a mimeographed exam-sheet that has fallen out of it.*) What are you doing with this exam, boning up for me?

GITTEL. Just looking.

JERRY. (*Scanning.*) '53, I'll have to go through this one tonight. (*He drops the novel and exam-sheet back on the bed, strips to the waist, now at last removes his hat and sets it on the desk-lamp, and collects the dirty plates and saucer of butts, while* GITTEL *watches him.*)

GITTEL. When you going to get some sleep? You're getting skinny!

JERRY. Muscle, I'm all muscle these days. And that reminds me, if you don't get off your rear end soon I'll be advertising in the Sunbathers Gazette for one that works. (*He bears the plates into the kitchen, where he next opens the oven and turns the steak over.*)

GITTEL. (*Scowling.*) Mine works.

JERRY. Unemployed. You think unemployed insurance can go on in perpetuity?

(*This is only kidding, while he proceeds to splash water into his face at the sink; but* GITTEL *staring into the future is so despondent she has to shake it off.*)

GITTEL. So when have you got any time, *now?*

JERRY. Three-thirty Friday after the battle, mother. Date?

GITTEL. In Central Park?

JERRY. (*Not hearing.*) And at your service, from then on in.

GITTEL. (*Glumly.*) For how long?

JERRY. Hey?

GITTEL. I said for how long.

JERRY. Can't hear you. (*He turns off the water and comes in, drying his face with a towel.*) Hm?

GITTEL. I said I love you. (JERRY *stands absolutely still for a long moment. Then* GITTEL *lowers her eyes.*) Hell, I don't have to say it, do I? You know it.

JERRY. (*Gently.*) Yes.

GITTEL. I'll try not to say it too often. Twice a week.

JERRY. You can't say it too often, it's part of my new muscle.

GITTEL. Maybe getting sick was the biggest favor I ever did you, huh?

JERRY. I think we can manage without. The big favor is to get back on your feet, Gittel. (GITTEL's *eyes are down.* JERRY *glances at his watch, bends to kiss her cheek, and crosses to the bureau.*)

GITTEL. (*Low.*) What's the percentage?

JERRY. (*Opening a drawer frowns. He then takes out a laundered shirt, removes the cardboard, and slips into the shirt.*) The percentage is one hundred.

GITTEL. I don't mean to get better, I mean—

JERRY. I know what you mean. When I said I'd like to look out for you what do you think *I* meant, a thirty-day option? (*Buttoning his shirt he goes back into the kitchen, where he turns the potatoes off and puts a plate in the oven to warm.*) You ready for lunch?

GITTEL. You eat already?

JERRY. I'll have to take a sandwich into the office. You wouldn't care to spring to your feet and run around the plate three times, work up an appetite? (*He waits on her in the doorway; she does not meet his eyes.*)

GITTEL. I got an appetite.

JERRY. Ahm. (*Presently he turns back into the kitchen, where he prepares a tray—tumbler of milk, paper napkin, silverware, and the meal on a plate.*)

GITTEL. You ought to have more than a sandwich, Jerry, you get sick too we'll really be up the goddam creek. Get a malted, too, huh? And tell him make it a guggle-muggle while he's at it.

JERRY. A what?

GITTEL. It's with a beat up egg. I mean two whole days of exam, you got to keep your strength up for those cruds.

JERRY. (*Brings in the tray, and places it on her lap in bed.*) The condemned man ate a hearty guggle-muggle and lived another thirty-four years. I don't intend to get sick, infant, even to get you up. (*He collects papers and books on the table, slipping them into his briefcase, and pauses over the legal document he has dropped there; he takes it up, and with his back to GITTEL reads it again, grimly.*)

GITTEL. Jerry.

JERRY. Yes.

GITTEL. (*Painfully.*) I'm not just taking advantage, you know, I'm—I mean since you been living here I'm—

Nobody ever took care of me so good, it sort of weakens your will-power, you know?

JERRY. (*Looks over his shoulder at her, then back to the document; he is deliberating between them.*) Strengthens mine.

GITTEL. I mean I'm kind of in the habit of—seeing your neckties around, now. I'll miss them.

JERRY. (*A silence,* JERRY *weighing the document and something else, much heavier, in himself. Then.*) Why do you think I'm taking this Bar exam, you boob, to lift legal dumbbells? I intend to live here, work here, be used. Lot of my life I've been cold from being unused.

GITTEL. I'm scared of afterwards, Jerry.

JERRY. What's afterwards?

GITTEL. I get up out of here, all the goddam neckties go back to your place. I'm scared to—live alone, again. Now.

JERRY. (*Stands for a long moment with the document. Then abruptly and decisively he wads it into his brief-case, sits, thrusts books and papers away to clear space, and writes.*) Eat your lunch.

GITTEL. (*Obeys, for a mouthful or two, but watches him perplexedly.*) What are you writing?

JERRY. A promissory note. I promise you, conversation at meals. (*When he is finished he folds the paper; standing, he takes up the gift box.*) And other items, less elevating. (*He lifts out a Chinese bed-jacket of brocaded silk.* GITTEL *drops her fork.*)

GITTEL. Hey! That's *beautiful*, what is it?

JERRY. Something to remember me by, till six o'clock.

GITTEL. A bed-jacket! Ye gods, I'll never get up. (*She wiggles her fingers for it, but* JERRY *holds up the folded paper.*)

JERRY. This is a letter to my landlord. (*He slips it into the pocket of the bed-jacket.*) For *you* to mail. By hand.

GITTEL. Huh?

JERRY. At the corner. As soon as you're on your feet to make it down there.

GITTEL. Why, what's it say? (*Her eyes widen.*) Get a new tenant! Huh?

JERRY. See for yourself.

GITTEL. You'll move the neckties in for keeps?

JERRY. See for yourself. (*From across the room he holds the bed-jacket ready for her, the letter poking out prominently.*)

GITTEL. (*Reproachfully.*) Jerry.

JERRY. Come and get it.

GITTEL. (*Reproachfully.*) Jerry, I got to be on my feet to get you?

JERRY. Maybe. Better find out, hm? (GITTEL *shakes her head.*) Is it so out of the question that I want to keep the goddam neckties here? Come on. (GITTEL *just gazes at him, her eyes moist.*) Come. Come and get it. (GITTEL *puts the tray aside, moves her legs to the edge, and sits still.*) Come on, honey.

GITTEL. (*Stands, unsteady for a moment, then moves toward him, afraid of her belly, afraid of her legs, the progress of someone who hasn't walked in a month; but she gets to him and the letter, unfolds it, and reads.*) You're giving up your flat.

JERRY. Save rent.

GITTEL. (*A pause.*) You're really ruining me, Jerry! (*She keeps her face averted, on the verge of tears.*) I didn't use to be a—bitch of a—lousy blackmailer. (*Another pause.*) And I'm not going to be either! Enough is enough! (*And with sudden resolution she tears the letter into pieces.*)

JERRY. (*Equably.*) That's how you waste forest resources? Now I'll have to write another.

GITTEL. Not unless you want to!

JERRY. I want to. (*His arms wrap her in the bed-jacket, and hold her. He kisses her, studies her eyes; she searches his. Then he glances at his watch, pats her cheek, and reaches for his brief-case.*) Don't overdo a good thing. Lie down soon. Chew your lunch before swallowing. Take your medicine. Don't tackle the stairs alone. Button up your overcoat, you belong to me. (*He is on his way to the door, when her small voice stops him.*)

GITTEL. Jerry. I do. You know I do, now?

JERRY. Yes. I know that, infant.

GITTEL. I love you. (JERRY *stands inarticulate, until she releases him:*) That's twice, there, I used up the whole week!

JERRY. (*Lightly.*) I may need to hear it again before that Bar exam. For muscle.

GITTEL. You'll pass.

JERRY. Hell, I'll blow all the answers out of my brilliant nose.

(*He blows her a kiss and is out the door, gone, leaving her on her feet in the room, shaking her head after him, in her Chinese silk, like a rainbow, half radiance, half tears. She fingers his coat, sits, and brings it to her face; she is much troubled.*)

## CURTAIN

## ACT THREE

### SCENE 2

*Jerry's room.*

*It is May, almost summer now, a hot muggy dusk, and eight months since this affair began. Once again the windows of both rooms are open—Jerry's from the top—and the sounds of TRAFFIC float in. In Gittel's room the only change is that the table is cleared of all Jerry's exam-preparations, the night-table is cleared of medicines, the bed is made. Jerry's flat, however, is a shambles. Packing is in progress, nothing is in its place, cartons stand here and there. In the kitchen JERRY in his shirt-sleeves is slowly wrapping dishware in newspaper; in the living room GITTEL—barefoot and back to normal, but*

*with a stratum of gloom underneath—is folding
linens into a carton. This separate activity goes on
for an interval of silence, until* JERRY *calls in; his
voice is rather dispirited, and so is hers.*

JERRY. What about these pots, honey? You want them
packed separate?
GITTEL. Separate from what?
JERRY. Dishes.
GITTEL. Guess so. I mean, sure. (*They go back to
packing in silence. Both are sweaty with the prosaic
drudgery of packing, and depressed, but neither is
admitting this; there is an atmosphere of something being
avoided. Then* GITTEL *stands on a chair to take down
the clothes-closet curtain, and in the process jogs one
support of the rod with its remaining clothes; it falls.*
GITTEL *grabs it.*) Help!
JERRY. (*Drops what he is doing, and comes at once,
on the run.*) What's wrong?
GITTEL. This cruddy pole. S'all.
JERRY. (*Relieved.*) Oh. I thought you— (*He stops
himself, takes the rod and clothes off her hands, and lays
them on the couch.*) Never did get around to fixing that
thing permanently. Guess I never believed it was perma-
nent, all it takes is two screws and a— (*He becomes
aware of her eyes moody on him.*) Hm?
GITTEL. Nothing.

(*They gaze at each other a moment, something unsaid
between them. Then* JERRY *grips her at the waist,
and lifts her down.*)

JERRY. You stay on the ground, squirrel.
GITTEL. (*Irked.*) Why?
JERRY. Because I've climbed Long's Peak four times.
I'm used to these rare altitudes. (*He climbs the chair,
and begins to unhook the curtain.*)
GITTEL. What'd you think, I was doing a nose dive?
No such luck.

JERRY. (*Another gaze.*) What kind of cheery remark is that?

GITTEL. I mean *bad* luck.

JERRY. Oh. I thought you meant good bad luck.

GITTEL. What's Long's Peak?

JERRY. Mountain. Front Range, Colorado. Fourteen thousand feet, up on all fours, down on all fives.

GITTEL. (*A pause.*) I been up the Empire State nineteen times, so what?

JERRY. (*Smiles, shakes his head, and turns to hand her the curtain.*) Here. (*But* GITTEL *is on her way out to the kitchen, in a mood.* JERRY *stares, tosses the curtain onto the couch mattress, bare in its ticking, and considers the window-drapes.*) You want this other one down?

GITTEL. (*Out of sight.*) What other one?

JERRY. Window curtain.

GITTEL. D'*you* want it down?

JERRY. (*Puzzled.*) Yes, I want it down.

GITTEL. So take it down!

JERRY. (*Frowning.*) What's eating you?

GITTEL. A banana!

JERRY. What?

GITTEL. A banana. (*She comes in again, eating a banana.*) Want a bite?

JERRY. I said, what's eating *you*. (*He moves the chair to the window, gets up again, and works on the burlap drapes.*)

GITTEL. Oh, *me*. What's eating you?

JERRY. I asked you first.

GITTEL. I mean what's eating me is figuring out what's eating you.

JERRY. I see. Well, what's eating me is figuring out what's eating you. Which just about exhausts that investigation. Be altogether fruitless except for the banana. Want these brackets too? (GITTEL *not replying bites at the banana, and* JERRY *looks from the brackets down to her.*) Hm?

GITTEL. *I* don't want a goddam thing. D'*you* want them?

JERRY. (*A pause.*) Correction. Do *we* want them?

GITTEL. We sure do. Cost good money, can always use them.

JERRY. That's right, ten cents a pair. I'll get a screwdriver. (*He comes down, to head for the kitchen.*)

GITTEL. So then don't!

JERRY. I mean what do we need *all* this junk for? We have your curtains there, we're not going to—

GITTEL. What junk? (*She is handling the drapes, pinches up a piece.*) That's good stuff, forty-seven cents a yard reduced, I could make eleven different things out of it.

JERRY. Name ten.

GITTEL. Anything. Bedspread, cushions, pocketbook, I was even thinking I'd make you some neckties.

JERRY. (*Very dubious.*) Well.

GITTEL. You don't want?

JERRY. I just don't see myself appearing in court in a red burlap necktie. (*He goes into the kitchen. GITTEL takes up the banana again for a last bite, slings the peel straight across the room out the open window, and sits gloomily on the couch. JERRY returning with the screwdriver studies her as he passes.*) Maybe we ought to knock off for tonight, infant. You look tired.

GITTEL. (*Testily.*) I'm not tired!

JERRY. Then why so down?

GITTEL. *Who's* down? I'm in sixth heaven! (*JERRY stops to eye her before mounting the chair.*) Just don't rush to the rescue. You're killing me with kindness.

JERRY. (*After a moment plunges the screw-driver by the handle straight into the chair, and lets it stand; GITTEL's eyes widen. But JERRY shows no further vehemence, and when he speaks it is calmly enough.*) That's in exchange for all the little needles.

GITTEL (*Sullen.*) I'm sorry.

JERRY. We're supposed to be joyfully packing to be together. Why act as though—

GITTEL. Nobody around here's *enjoying* this. Every frigging towel I put in that box I feel worse.

JERRY. (*Dryly.*) It's a chore, who likes to break up a happy home? (*He fishes in his shirt-pocket for cigarettes.*) Though in a peculiar way it has been. I won't forget *this* first-aid station in a hurry.

GITTEL. There's always the next one.

JERRY. What next one?

GITTEL. The one we're fixing up for me. (JERRY *looks at her, lights the cigarette, and to avoid the topic mounts the chair again with the screw-driver.* GITTEL *takes a fresh breath and dives in, very brightly.*) Look, Jerry, whyn't we just, sort of, get married and get the goddam thing over with, huh?

JERRY. (*Half-turns, to gaze at her over his shoulder.*) Bigamy? Big of you, I mean, I have one wife now.

GITTEL. I mean *after* the divorce. I'm not going to be just a ball and chain, now you passed that Bar exam you know the first thing I'm going to do? Take up shorthand!

JERRY. Shorthand is the one thing this romance has lacked from the beginning.

GITTEL. So when you open your law-office, there I am! A goddam secretary, you're really going to save dough on me. And soon as I make enough out of that loft I'm going to fix up the flat for us, real nice.

JERRY. It's real nice.

GITTEL. Stinks.

JERRY. What stinks about it?

GITTEL. It's a dump, you think I don't know that? My God, how can you entertain somebody a cockroach committee comes out of the sink to see who's here? Hasn't been an exterminator in there since Babe Ruth.

JERRY. Who are we exterminating?

GITTEL. Huh?

JERRY. I meant to say entertaining.

GITTEL. Well, anybody you need to. Customers! Partners, the Taubmans, maybe *criminals,* you don't know who yet, but you can't have a dump for them. Can you?

JERRY. (*A pause.*) No. I couldn't think of representing some dope-addict who'd just murdered his mother and have him see a cockroach. Here's the brackets. (*But* GITTEL *is folding the drapes to put in the carton, and he steps down with them.*)

GITTEL. Who knows, maybe later on we'll move to a real apartment-house even. You know one thing I always wanted to live in a house with?

JERRY. Me?

GITTEL. An elevator! With an elevator you can invite anybody.

JERRY. (*Drops the brackets in her purse, next to her little radio. The radio stops him, he contemplates it, rubs it with his thumb, and then finds* GITTEL'S *eye on him. Smiles.*) Remembering the day you left this at the door. We kept each other company many a wee hour, I hate to see it end up all alone in some closet.

GITTEL. Nah, we'll use it.

JERRY. (*Mildly.*) If you have in mind plastic neckties, they're also out. I have room for it in with the pots.

(*He takes the radio out into the kitchen.* GITTEL *on her knees begins on another carton, loading in books, papers, a miscellany.*)

GITTEL. (*Calling out.*) What about this stuff, Jerry, bills? Gas, phone—

JERRY. (*Out of sight.*) Leave them out where I'll see them, I don't think I paid those yet.

GITTEL. (*Discarding them.*) What do you want to pay them, all they can do is shut it off if you do or you don't. Letters— (*She unfolds one, on feminine blue stationery.*) "Jerry dearest, I—" Whoops. (*She shuts it in a hurry, not reading it, but as she puts it away she comes to a legal document in blue backing that tickles her memory: the last time she saw it was in her room, in* JERRY'S *hands. She reads, frowning, her lips moving at first soundlessly, then becoming audible.*) "—although the plaintiff has conducted herself as a true and faithful wife to the defendant, the said defendant has been guilty. Of acts of cruelty toward the plaintiff, destroying the—"

(*Now* JERRY *is standing in the doorway, a cup in his hand.*) "—peace of mind of the plaintiff and the objects of—matrimony. It is hereby ordered, adjudged—"

JERRY. (*Completes it from memory. Slowly.*) —and decreed by the Court that the bonds of matrimony heretofore existing are severed and held for naught. And that the said plaintiff is granted an absolute divorce from the defendant. Unquote.

GITTEL. (*After a silence.*) So why didn't you tell me, Jerry?

JERRY. (*A pause.*) I had to live with it. A while longer. Digest it. Let it grow out with my fingernails, till I was— rid of it.

GITTEL. (*Another pause.*) You didn't want me to know.

JERRY. Not till I was—on top of it. Do you know what the sense of never is? Never again, not even once? Never is a deep hole, it takes time to—close over.

GITTEL. Then what'll you do?

JERRY. Then?

GITTEL. Yeah. Then.

JERRY. (*A pause, gently.*) I think I'll do one thing at a time.

GITTEL. What?

JERRY. Pack this cup. (*He comes to the carton with it, kneeling near her.*)

GITTEL. You sonofabitch. (JERRY *wheels on his knee to confront her.*) You tell her about *me*? That you moved in?

JERRY. (*Whitely.*) Yes.

GITTEL. Because I had a hemorrhage?

JERRY. I'm *not* a sonofabitch—

GITTEL. *Did you tell her I had a hemorrhage?*

JERRY. Yes.

GITTEL. And you didn't tell me about this? (*She slings the decree straight into his face.* JERRY *squats, rigid.* GITTEL *then scrambles up and makes for her shoes.* JERRY *rising slams the cup into the carton of crockery.*) Smash them all, who needs them?

JERRY. What are you off on this time?

GITTEL. I'm getting out of here, you—you goddam— (*But the grief breaks through, and she wails to him out of loss:*) Jerry, *why* didn't you *tell* me?

JERRY. I couldn't.

GITTEL. (*Gazing at him, she takes this in; then she finishes putting her shoes on, and makes a bee-line for her bag.*) Yeah. You only tell her about me. My God, even when you *divorce* her it's a secret you have with her! One of these days you'll marry me, she'll know it and I won't! (*But when she turns to the doorway,* JERRY *is planted in it, blocking her.*)

JERRY. You're not leaving.

GITTEL. Jerry, look out!

JERRY. Sit down.

GITTEL. You look out or I'll let you have it, Jerry!

JERRY. Go ahead, street brawler. (GITTEL *slaps him across the face, he is unmoving; she slaps him again back-hand, he is like a statue, she then wheels looking for a weapon, comes up from the carton with the broken cup, and charges his face, but hesitates.* JERRY *stands moveless. waiting.*) Do. I'll beat your behind off.

GITTEL. (*Flinging the cup past him, she throws herself averted on the couch, tearful with rage.*) Sonofabitch, all my life I never yet could beat up one goddam man, it's just *no* fair!

JERRY. Why do you think I told her about the hemorrhage?

GITTEL. To prove something to her on *me*, now.

JERRY. Like what?

GITTEL. How you're so wonderful, looking after me, you don't need her help.

JERRY. I told her because she asked *my* help. She wants me home.

GITTEL. (*Rolls over, to stare at him.*) She does?

JERRY. When at last she really needs me, and I'm enough my own man to help, I had to say no. And why.

GITTEL. (*A deep breath.*) Okay, Jerry. You said make a claim, right?

JERRY. Yes.

GITTEL. So I'm going to make it.

JERRY. All right.

GITTEL. I want you here. I want *all* of you here. I don't want half a hunk of you, I want—I mean it's—(*With difficulty.*) It's leap year, Jerry, tell the truth. *Would* you—ever say—I love you? Once.

JERRY. (*Pained.*) It's a lifetime promise, infant, I've only said it once. (*But the moment he turns again to the kitchen, her voice rises after him:*)

GITTEL. Jerry, Jerry, give me a break, will you? Don't kid me along. Is that a friend? (*This word nails him, he turns back with his eyes moist.*) I'll tell you straight, you move in I just—won't give up on you marrying me. You—you let me have it straight, too. (*He stands, gazing at her.*) Jerry, you my friend?

JERRY. (*Finally.*) I'm your friend. Here it is, straight. You say love, I think you mean *in* love. I mean so much more by that word now—

GITTEL. I mean wanting. Somebody. So bad—

JERRY. Not wanting. Love is having, having had, having had so—deeply, daily, year in and out, that a man and woman exchange—guts, minds, memories, exchange—eyes. Love is seeing through the other's eyes. So because she likes bridges I never see a bridge here without grief, that her eyes are not looking. A hundred things like that. Not simply friend, some ways my mortal enemy, but *wife,* and ingrown. (*He looks down at the decree.*) What *could* I tell you about this—piece of paper, that the bonds of matrimony are *not* severed? Why would I—love my right hand, if I lost it? That's what love is. To me, now.

GITTEL. (*Keeps her eyes on him for a long moment, then she closes them.*) You ever tell her that?

JERRY. No. I should have told her years ago, I didn't know it then.

GITTEL. (*Rolls up; she climbs the chair at the window and hangs gazing out, to find her way through this.*) You'll never marry me, Jerry.

JERRY. I can't, infant.

GITTEL. So what kind of competition can I give her, have a hemorrhage twice a year? Trap you that way, be *more* of a cripple, one month to another? Get half of you by being a wreck on your hands, will that keep you around?

JERRY. As long as you need me, I'll be around.

GITTEL. (*Turns on the chair, staring at him, as it dawns on her.*) And you'll move in. Even now.

JERRY. What's in me to give, without short-changing, I'll give—

GITTEL. My God, *I'm* in a goddam trap! (*A pause; then* JERRY *nods.*) You're one, all right, I could—lose a leg or something in you.

JERRY. Yes, you could lose—a lot of time. You're a growing girl, and of the two things I really want, one is to see you grow. And bear your fruit.

GITTEL. And the other is—

JERRY. Tess.

GITTEL. Jerry, Jerry, Jerry. (*She regards him, her eyes blinking; this is hard to say.*) I don't *want* the short end. I want somebody'll—say to me what you just said about her. (*She gets down, retrieves her bag, and stands not looking at him.*) What do you say we—give each other the gate, huh, Jerry? (*She moves to pass him in the doorway; but he stops her, to take her face between his palms, and search her eyes.*)

JERRY. For whose sake?

GITTEL. Jerry, I haven't taken one happy breath since that hemorrhage, I want to get out of here and *breathe*.

(*After a moment* JERRY *lets her go. She brushes quickly past him, through the kitchen and out of the flat. He turns in the doorway, looking after her, with his hands up on the jambs, unmoving as the LIGHTS dim.*)

*CURTAIN*

## ACT THREE

### SCENE 3

*Both rooms.*

*It is a few days later, a gray afternoon. Jerry's room is altogether cleaned out, bare except for his suitcase and portable typewriter standing there, and the phone on the floor near them. JERRY is not in sight, though we may hear him in the kitchen. GITTEL is in her room, taking the dance-photos of herself down from the wall. She is engaged in this without feeling, almost without awareness; it is something to do while she waits. What she is waiting for is the phone, as we see from her eyes. She takes the photos to her night-table and drops them in a drawer, then walks nervously round and round her room, eyeing her alarm-clock, eyeing her phone. Meanwhile a match has been lighted in JERRY'S dark kitchen, JERRY making a last survey of it. When he comes in, he is in street-clothes and hat; he is shaking the match out, his other arm cradles a few last toilet articles, shaving-cream, brush, razor. He kneels at the typewriter case, and fits these articles carefully in. Then he consults his wristwatch. He stands over the phone a heavy moment, picks it up, and dials. The PHONE in GITTEL's room rings, and she flies to sit on her bed on it.*

GITTEL. Yeah, hello?

JERRY. (*A pause.*) Honey, I'm—all packed here, I—

GITTEL. (*Softly.*) Hiya, Jerry.

JERRY. (*A pause.*) Some cartons of—odds and ends in the kitchen here, the key will be with the janitor. If you want anything.

GITTEL. I won't want anything.

JERRY. If you do. (*A pause.*) Look, if you do, I mean anything—important, Gittel, I'm at the Commodore Hotel in Lincoln, I don't have the number, long-distance will give it to you. Lincoln, Nebraska. *Not* Nevada.

GITTEL. Not Nevada.

JERRY. And not Omaha, I'm not walking back into that mistake, ever again. As soon as I get an office and a phone I'll send you the number. Now if you—if you need anything in a hurry, I mean instantly, will you call Frank Taubman? You won't have to explain anything, it's taken care of, just call him.

GITTEL. (*A pause.*) Yeah.

JERRY. No. Promise.

GITTEL. I promise. (*A pause.*) Jerry, I'm all right now. You just—you just get what you want out there, huh?

JERRY. I'll try. It's back to the wars. My terms are steep, I won't work for Lucian, I won't live in Omaha, and all we'll have is what I earn. I'm beginning very— modestly, a desk and a phone and a pencil. And what's in my head.

GITTEL. It's a lot.

JERRY. But I won't short-change her. It has to be a new deal, on both sides.

GITTEL. I'm rooting for you, Jerry.

JERRY. No backsliding. By you either, Gittel, don't you give up either, hm?

GITTEL. Oh, I don't! I bounce up, like a—jack in a box, you know?

JERRY. I'm rooting for you too. It's a big city and you're the salt of the earth, just don't waste it, he's around some corner. You'll find him.

GITTEL. I'm looking. I got a better opinion of myself now, I'm going to propose more often. I'll send you a birthday card now and then, huh?

JERRY. Now and then.

GITTEL. Twice a week!

JERRY. (*Pinches his eyes; he is shaky.*) Gittel. What am I doing, I—moments here I think I—

GITTEL. You're doing right, Jerry. I mean *I* don't want any handouts either, you know? That's no favor.

JERRY. If I know anything I know that.

GITTEL. And I'm not going to be just giving them out, from now on. I want somebody'll take care of me who's all mine. You taught me that. And nobody like Sam or Jake, between them they couldn't take care of a chiclet. I mean, things look a lot different to me, Jerry, you did me a world of good.

JERRY. Did I really? Golly, if I could think each of us—helped somehow, helped a bit—

GITTEL. You been a great help, Jerry, it's the first affair I—come out with more than I went in. I mean, wherever this guy is, he'll owe you!

JERRY. (*A pause, humbly.*) Thank you for that. And she'll owe you more than she'll know. After— (*He tries to recall it.*) After the verb to love, to help is—

GITTEL. (*A pause.*) What, Jerry?

JERRY. —the sweetest in the tongue. Somebody said it. Well. (*He looks at his watch.*) Well. So long, infant.

GITTEL. (*She tries to say it, but her eyes are full, her heart is in her mouth, and she struggles to keep it from overflowing there; she cannot.*) I love you, Jerry! (JERRY *is rigid; it takes her a moment to go on.*) Long as you *live* I want you to remember the last thing you heard out of me was I love you!

JERRY. (*Long pause.*) I love you too, Gittel.

(*He hangs up, and for a moment there is no movement. Then* JERRY *puts the phone down, and lights himself a cigarette; his first drag tells us how much he needs it. After another, he kneels again, shuts the typewriter case, stands with it and the suitcase in either hand, and gives the room a final check.* GITTEL *meanwhile has not hung up; she clicks down, then rapidly dials again. But the minute it rings once, she claps it down.* JERRY *is on his way out with typewriter and suitcase when the single RING comes. He stops, not putting either down, just staring at the phone for a long minute.* GITTEL *sits, head high, eyes closed. Neither moves. Then* GITTEL *takes her hand off the phone. And* JERRY *turns, and walks out of his flat.*)

*END OF THE PLAY*

## TWO FOR THE SEESAW

### LIGHT CUES

#### *ACT ONE*

SCENE 1: LATE AFTERNOON—Both Sets.
    Gittel's Apartment, brighter.
 1. Dim Up Sky—Then HIS Apartment.
    Kitchen Lite On.
 2. Dim Up HER Apartment.
 3. Dim Out Both Sets.

SCENE 2: MIDNIGHT—Gittel's Apartment.
 4. Dim Up Hall Lights and Window.
 5. Bump On—Living Room Lamp.
 6. Bump On—Kitchen Lamp.
 7. Bump On—Back Room.
 8. Bump Off—Living Room Lamp.
 9. Bump Off—Back Room.
 10. Dim Out HER Set (Follow Spot last).

SCENE 3: DAWN INTO DAY—Both Sets.
 11. Dim Up HIS Set, Kitchen Lite On.
 12. Dim Up HER Set.
 13. Dim Down Both Sets.
 14. Balcony Out on Curtain.

#### *ACT TWO*

SCENE 1: OCTOBER, LATE AFTERNOON—Jerry's
    Apartment.
 15. Dim Up Sky—then HIS Apartment Kitchen
    Lite On. Lamp On.
 16. Bump Off—Living Room Lamp.
 17. Dim Down—Exterior and Interior (2 min.).
 18. Bump Off—Candle.
 19. Bump On—Living Room Lamp.
 20. Bump Off—Living Room Lamp.
 21. Dim Out—HIS Set.

Scene 2: DECEMBER, NOON—Both Sets.
    22. Dim Up Both Sets (Gittel's Heater On).
    23. Dim Out Both Sets.

Scene 3: FEBRUARY, MIDNIGHT—Gittel's Apartment.
    24. Dim Up Hall, Window and Back Lights.
    25. Bump On—Kitchen Light.
    26. Bump On—Living Room Lamp.
    27. Bump Off—Living Room Lamp.
    28. Bump On—Gas Heater.
    29. Bump On—Living Room Lamp.
    30. Bump Off—Living Room Lamp.
    31. Bump On—Living Room Lamp.
    32. Dim Down HER Set.

*ACT THREE*

Scene 1: MARCH, NOON, BRIGHT—Gittel's Apartment.
    33. Dim Up Sky—then HER Apartment.
    34. Dim Out—(around Gittel—Follow Spot last)

Scene 2: MAY, DUSK—Jerry's Apartment.
    35. Dim Up HIS Set.
    36. Dim Down—Exterior and Interior.
    37. Dim Out HIS Set.

Scene 3: MAY, GRAY AFTERNOON—Both Sets.
    38. Dim Up Both Sets.
    39. Dim Down Both Sets.
    40. Balcony Out on Curtain

TWO FOR THE SEESAW

## ELECTRIC FIXTURES

*GITTEL'S APARTMENT:*

    *Living Room:* Chinese Lantern—on Wall Left of Bed.
    Gas Heater—up Right Corner of Bed.

    Phone (Modern, Bells in Base)—on Night Table.

    *Kitchen:* Lamp (Lumiline)—above Stove under Cabinet.

    Frypan (Milk Boil Effect)—In Range.

    Sink (Gravity Fed from 5 gal. Tank in Back room).

    Stove (Lumiline Light in Oven and one Burner on Range).

*JERRY'S APARTMENT:*

    *Living Room:* Chinese Lantern—on Wall above Bed (Act 2)

    Candle (Battery)—on Dining Table (Act 2).

    Phone (Modern, Bells in Base).

    *Kitchen:* Lamp (Bracket)—Wall Left of Door.
    (Lumiline in Transom works with it.
    For N. Y. Production only.
    Necessary for set identification.)

# TWO FOR THE SEESAW

## PROPERTY PLOT

### *JERRY'S APARTMENT*
### *ACT ONE*

*Living Room*
Day Bed (Unmade)
Chair
Light Fixture L. Wall
*On Bed*
Sheets (2)
Blanket
Pillow w/case
Sunday Times (7 sections)
Suitcase w/Suit Coat on Hanger
*On Chair*
Coffee Pot w/coffee
Cup & Saucer (also used in 32)
Small Plate (also used in 32)
*By Bed*
Telephone (Electrics)
Phone Book
Ash Tray
*In Closet*
2 Sport Coats on Hangers
Suit Coat on Hanger (Costume)
Doweling (rigged to fall on cue)
*On Window*
Suit Pants on Hanger
Fake Glass in Window

*On Light Fixture*
Shirt on Hanger
Jerry's Hat (Costume)
*Kitchen*
Sink
Stove w/Oven above it
Tub w/cover
*On Stove*
2 Pot Holders (Pre-Set for 21)
*In Oven*
Chicken Casserole, not eaten (Pre-Set for 21)
Potatoes in a Bowl, eaten (Sliced apples—Pre-Set 21)
*By Sink*
Hammer
*Personal*
Empty Cigarette Pack (Jerry)
Bandage for hand (Jerry) Pre-Set in Suit Coat for 21)
*Off Left*
Telegram (Set in 12 for 13)
Chimes (13)
Card Table: w/(21) Table Cloth

92

2 Plates w/pears
2 Sets of Silverware
2 Mugs
2 Napkins
Food Tongs
Salad Fork and Spoon
Cigarette Jar w/5 Cigs.
Matches
Ash Tray
Candle (electrics)
Small Phone Table: w/
    (21)
    Ash Tray
    Cloth
Bookcase (2 shelf): w/
    (21)
    Gittel's Brown Purse
    (Duplicate of one off
    Right)
2 Kitchen Shelves: w/
    (21)
    Health Bread (eaten)
    Salt & Pepper Shakers
Refrigerator: w/(21)
    Bottle of Wine (used)
    Salad Dressing
Painted Chair (21)
Painted Half-Chair (21)
Window Drapes (21)
Rod w/removable brackets
    to hold drapes (21)
Closet Curtain on Wire
    (21)
Coat Hanger
Cork Screw (21)
Briefcase (Jerry's — used
    in 21, 22, 31)
2 Law Books (21)

Small Brown Bag (Thread
    not opened (21)
White Bag (Bakery—not
    opened) (21)
Gift Bag w/Boxed Cha-
    nel Soap (21)
Key Ring w/Keys (22)
Heater (22)
Three Letters
    (Jerry) — not opened
    (22)
Blue Feminine Letter
    (opened) (22)
Legal Paper (22)
Banana (32)
Gas Bill (32)
Phone Bill (32)
Divorce Decree (Duplicate
    of one Off R.—32)
Blue Feminine Letter
    (Duplicate of one in 22)
8 Letters (32)
Bath Towel (32)
Bed Spread for Day Bed
    (21)
Screwdriver (32)
Sauce Pan (32)
Newspapers (for wrap-
    ping) (32)
Cardboard Carton (with
    paper and broken china
    for crash of cup) (32)
4 Cardboard Cartons (32)
3 Cardboard Cartons
    Fastened together in a
    stack (32)
Portable Typewriter
Suitcase (Duplicate of one

used in 11 and Off Right
(32)
Shaving Brush

Razor
Shaving Cream in a Tube

## ACT TWO

*Strike*
Suitcase
Chair
Pillow
Sheets
Blanket
Newspaper
Broken Glass
*Set*
Bed Spread on Day Bed
Bookcase w/Set Up
Radio from Gittel's Apart-
   ment on Bookcase
Phone Table w/Set Up
Telephone on Phone table
Chair
½ Chair
Card Table w/Set Up
Closet Curtain on Wire
Coat Hanger on Doweling
   in Closet
Sport Coat (Costume) w/
   Legal Paper in pocket
   in Closet (Pre-Set for
   22)

Keys on Door Frame
   (Pre-Set for 22)
Window Drapes on Rod
Kitchen Shelves on Right
   Wall above sink in
   Kitchen w/bread and
   salt shaker
Ice-box w/wine and salad
   dressing
Corkscrew on Tub
Salad in Bowl on Tub
*Check*
French Frieds & Chicken
   Casserole in Oven
2 Pot Holders on Stove
Jerry's Hand Props Off L.:
   Briefcase
   2 Law Books
   Brown Bag
   White Bag
   Gift Bag w/soap
   3 Letters (Pre-Set for
      22)
   Blue Feminine Letter
      (pre-set for 22)

## ACT THREE

*Strike*
Bookcase
Heater
Phone Table
3 Paper Bags from
   Kitchen
Bed Spread

Wall Decoration
Fruit Bowl
*Set*
Folded Sheets on Bed
   (from Act I)
Folded Blanket on Bed
   (from Act I)

Bath Towel on Bed
Gittel's Tote Bag D. C.
(Identical one to Off R.)
Gittel's Brown Purse D. C.
Empty Carton D. C.w/
under it:
Gas Bill
Phone Bill
Divorce Decree
8 Letters
Blue Feminine Letter
Crash Box D. C.
Gittel's Shoes (Costume)
by Pipe by Window
3 Cartons by Tub
Screw Driver on Tub
Newspapers on Tub
1 Cup and 2 Saucers
(from Act I) on Tub

Sauce Pan on Tub
Empty Carton on Tub
Banana in Ice-box
Typewriter (open) in
Closet (pre-set for 33)
Suitcase in Closet (pre-set
for 33)
Shave Cream, Razor,
Brush on Kitchen Sink
(pre-set for 33)
2 Empty Cartons off Door-
way
*Move*
Radio to D. S. Foot of Bed
on Floor
½ Chair L. C.
Chair above Bed
*Strike*
All Dressing for Act II

*During Blackout for 33*

*Strike*
Bed
½ Chair

Crash Box
Chair
Divorce Decree

# DRESSING LIST

## *JERRY'S APARTMENT*

*In Kitchen (Act I)*
Pair of Socks on Hanger
    on Light Fixture
*In Living Room (Act II)*
Area Rug
*On Bed*
5 Throw Pillows
*On Bookcase*
Plant
Books on Shelves
*Over Bed on Wall*
2 Pictures
Chinese Lantern

*In Closet*
Suit Coat
*In Kitchen*
Cloth Skirt under Sink
Boxed and Canned Goods
    on Shelves
Spice Rack on Wall under
    Light Fixture
Basket of Fruit on Refrig-
    erator
Soap Powder, Cleanser &
    Sugar Bowl on Shelf
    over Tub

# PROPERTY PLOT

## *GITTEL'S APARTMENT*

## *ACT ONE*

*Living Room*
Rugs (2)
Night Table
Heater
Bed
Chest
Sewing Machine
Sewing Chair
Waste Basket
Dress Form
Sling Chair
*On Night Table*
Telephone (Electrics)
Clock
Address Book
Pad
Pencil
*On Bed*
Sheets (2)
Pillows w/cases (2)
Blanket
Spread
Hot Water Bottle
    (under Blanket)
*On Chest*
Radio
Pajamas (in bottom
    drawer
*On Machine*
Scissors
Ash Tray w/butts

*On Dummy*
Bodice
Pin Cushion w/pins
*On Window Shelf*
Plant
*In Sling Chair*
Pillows (5)
*Outside Window*
Green Tree
*Kitchen*
Cabinets
Stove (Practical-Electrics)
Sink (Practical-Electrics)
Towel Racks (2)
Refrigerator
*On Stove*
Saucepan
Fry Pan (Electrics-Boiled
    Milk Effect)
Pan (in Oven) (Pre-Set
    for 31)
*In Cabinet*
4 Mugs (3 Pre-Set for 12)
1 Cup (Pre-Set for 23)
    (Broken each perform-
    ance)
Matches (hanging on side
    of cabinet)
Box of Cookies
Box of Matzos
Plastic Glass (Pre-Set for

97

23) (Broken each performance)

*On Refrigerator*

Tray (Pre-Set for 31)

Quart of Milk (inside ref.)

*On Sink*

Hand Towel (hanging on rack)
(Pre-Set for 31)

Can Opener, Spoon, Tongs (Pre-Set for 31)

Drain Pan (under sink) (Electrics)

Pot Holder (hanging on wall-rack)

*In Back Room*

Chair

Gittel's Wrapper (Costume)

Towels (2)

Gittel's Rain Coat (Costume) (Pre-Set for 22)

Pillow w/case (Pre-Set for 12)

Water Tank for Sink (Electrics)

*Off Right*

Tote Bag w/tights

Bag of Milk

2 Keys on Door (11, 23)

Black Purse (Gittel—12)

Carton of Coke (12)

Carton of Beer (12)

Cigar (12)

Door Slam (12)

Bare Tree (22, 23)

Brown Purse w/pills (Gittel—23)

Face Cream (22)

New Radio (22, 23, 31, 33)

Snow Windows (22, 23)

New Dress for Dummy (22, 23)

Newspaper (23)

Goose-necked Lamp (31)

2 Law Books (31)

Notes (31)

Thumb Tacks (31)

Novel w/Bar Exam. (31)

Legal Pad w/Pen (31)

Bed Pan (31)

Soiled Plate and Cup (31)

Dinner Plate (31)

Knife and Fork (31)

Glass (31)

Groceries (Steak and Potatoes in bag—31)

Suitcase w / clean shirt (Duplicate of one off Left—31)

Gift Box w/Bed Jacket (31)

Cheque (31)

Rack of 6 Ties (31)

Pants on Hanger (31)

Mail—
Harpers
Hospital Bill
Divorce Decree (Duplicate of one off Left—31)

## ACT TWO

*Strike*
Green Tree
Soiled Pan from Stove
Bodice from Dummy
Gittel's Black Purse
Tights
Hot Water Bottle
Coke and Beer Cartons
Soiled Mugs
*Move*
Make Bed
Close Windows
Pillows to Bed
Clock to Night Table
Ash Tray to Machine
Gittel's Wrapper to Off R.

*Set*
New Radio on Chest
New Dress on Dummy
Clean Pan on Stove (23)
Newspaper on Machine
 (23)
Bare Tree
Snow Windows
*Check*
Address Book on Night
 Table
Milk in Refrigerator
Tote Bag in Back Room
Face Cream off Right
Cup in Cabinet
Plastic Glass in Cabinet
Key on Door

## ACT THREE

*Strike*
Bare Tree
Snow Windows
Dummy
Newspaper
Broken Glass
Soiled or Broken Cup
Bottle of Pills
Gittel's Brown Purse
Soiled Pan
Gittel's Shoes from under
 Bed
Gittel's Blouse
*Move*
Clock to Chest
Milk to Refrigerator
*Set*
Green Tree

Notes on Uprights w/tacks
Goose-necked Lamp on
 Machine
Legal Pad w/Pen on
 Machine
Ash Tray w/butts on
 Machine
Grey Coat (Jerry's from
 Left Side) on back of
 chair
Dinner Plate on Stove
Soiled Plate and Cup on
 Chest
Novel w/Bar Exam on
 Chest
Pants on Hanger on Shut-
 ter
Rack of 6 Ties on Shelf sr

Bed Pan by Night Table
Suitcase w/Clean Shirt R. of Night Table
Glass on Refrigerator
Knife and Fork on Refrigerator
*Check*
Jerry's Briefcase off Right (from Jerry's Apartment)
2 Law Books off Right
Paper Bag w/Steak and Potatoes Off Right
Bed Jacket in Box off Right
Letters (Harpers, Hospital Bill, Divorce Decree) off Right
Cheque off Right
Can Opener, Tongs, Drain Spoon on Sink
Broil Pan in Oven
Clean Pan hanging from Stove
Hand Towel by Sink
Tray on Refrigerator
*Dressing*
Law Books (5) on Night Table and on Chest
Medicine Bottles (4) on Night Table

## *DURING 32*

*Strike*
All Books of Law
Notes from Posts
Legal Pad w/Pen from Machine
Medicine Bottles
Ties
Pants
Grey Coat
Bed Pan from Back Room
Soiled Pan on Stove
Jerry's Suitcase
Letters
Tray w/Dishes
Goose-necked Lamp from Machine
Gift Box
*Move*
Clock to Night Table
Empty Waste Basket
Make Bed
Cafe Curtains on Window close
Doors closed

# DRESSING LIST

## *GITTEL'S APARTMENT*

*On Wall Down Right*
Print
Wall Plate
2 Small Framed Pictures
Print
*On Shelves Over Heater*
Ceramic Pitcher
Dancing Figure
Ceramic Vase
Flower Pot
Ash Tray
Ceramic Fish
Books
*On Wall Over Chest*
4 Photos of "Gittel" Dancing
*On Wall Right of Window*
2 Photos of "Gittel" and "Larry"
2 Small Prints

*On Window*
Cafe Curtains
*Over Stove*
2 Small Fry Pans
1 Small Saucepan
*On Stove*
Kettle
*Over Refrigerator*
Hand Painted Sugar Bowl and 2 Blue Cannisters
Hand Painted Glass
Salt Shaker
Dish Cloth on Rack
*In Back Room*
2 Travel Posters on Wall
*On Night Table*
2 Small Books
Ash Tray
Matches
*On Chest*
Box of Kleenex

# TWO FOR THE SEESAW

## *COSTUME PLOT*

### *JERRY*

#### ACT ONE

SCENE 1:
  Gray sweater—coat style
  Gray pants
  Blue striped shirt
  Blue tie
  Black loafers

#### CHANGE TO

  Gray suit coat
  Hat

SCENE 2:
  Same as Change 11

SCENE 3:
  Same as Change 11

#### ACT TWO

SCENE 1:
  Hat
  Top coat
  Gray slacks
  Light gray tweed sport coat
  Brown shoes
  White shirt
  Blue tie

SCENE 2: Same as above except brown sport coat

SCENE 3:
  Hat
  Tan overcoat
  Blue suit
  Black shoes
  White shirt
  Blue tie

## ACT THREE

SCENE 1:
    Hat
    Gray tweed sport coat
    Gray slacks
    Blue striped shirt
    Black shoes
    Dark figured tie
                    CHANGE TO
    White shirt
                    CHANGE TO
    Blue tie
SCENE 2:
    White shirt
    Blue tie
    Gray slacks
    Black shoes
SCENE 3:
    Gray suit
    Hat
    Black shoes

## *GITTEL*
## ACT ONE

SCENE 1:
    Green, heavy knit sweater
    Red and olive houndstooth wool skirt
    Black stockings
    Black "elf" shoes
    White bra
    Black ½-slip
SCENE 2:
    Plum Paisley wool top
    Red wool skirt
    Black stockings
    Black flats
    Black leather belt
                    CHANGE TO
    Black and white striped pajamas
SCENE 3:
    Pajamas

## ACT TWO

SCENE 1:

Pink oxford shirt
Act 1, Scene 1 skirt
Brown belt
Black stockings
Black flats
Aqua striped tea towel

SCENE 2:

Green and blue plaid wrapper
Tape measure "belt"
Blue mules

### CHANGE TO

Rain Coat
Black stockings
Black flats

SCENE 3:

Flowered scarf
Black "fur" topper
Black skirt with red trim
White peasant blouse
Black stockings
Black flats

## ACT THREE

SCENE 1:

Pink flannel nightgown

SCENE 2:

Yellow and white striped blouse
Yellow skirt
Hose
Blue flats

SCENE 3:

Blue and pink plaid chiffon dress
Hose
Blue flats

*During Blackout for 22*

*Strike*
Card Table w/Set Up
*Set*
Heater

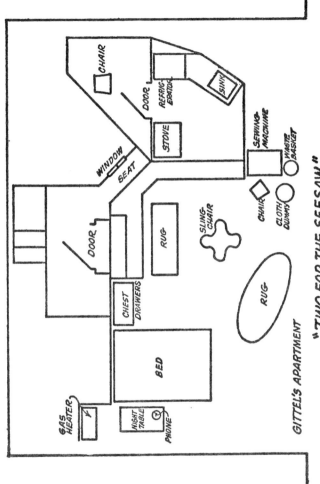

CHAIR

DOOR

REFRIG-
ERATOR

SINK

STOVE

WINDOW

SEAT

SEWING-
MACHINE

WASTE
BASKET

DOOR

RUG

SLING-
CHAIR

CHAIR

CLOTH
DUMMY

CHEST
DRAWERS

RUG

BED

GAS
HEATER

NIGHT
TABLE

PHONE

"TWO FOR THE SEESAW"

GITTEL'S APARTMENT

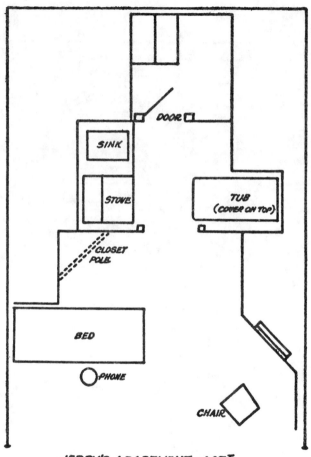

JERRY'S APARTMENT – ACT I
"TWO FOR THE SEESAW"

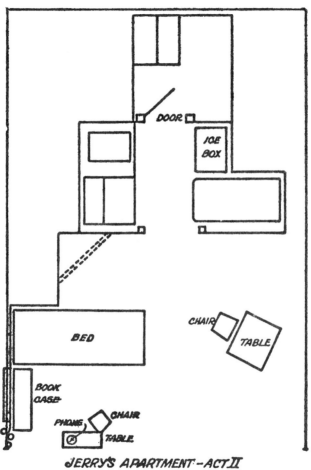

DOOR

ICE
BOX

BED

CHAIR

TABLE

BOOK
CASE

PHONE    CHAIR

TABLE

JERRY'S APARTMENT - ACT II
"TWO FOR THE SEESAW"

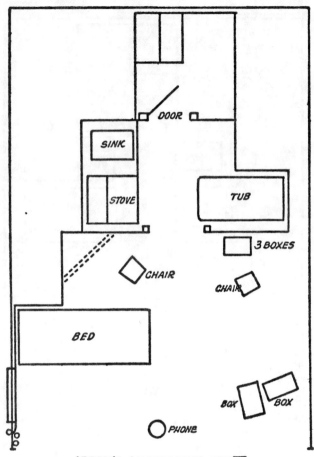

SINK

STOVE

DOOR

TUB

3 BOXES

CHAIR

CHAIR

BED

BOX

BOX

PHONE

JERRY'S APARTMENT – ACT III

"TWO FOR THE SEESAW"

# 6 RMS RIV VU
## BOB RANDALL
### (Little Theatre) Comedy
4 Men, 4 Women, Interior

A vacant apartment with a river view is open for inspection by prospective tenants, and among them are a man and a woman who have never met before. They are the last to leave and, when they get ready to depart, they find that the door is locked and they are shut in. Since they are attractive young people, they find each other interesting and the fact that both are happily married adds to their delight of mutual, yet obviously separate interests.

> ". . . a Broadway comedy of fun and class, as cheerful as a rising souffle. A sprightly, happy comedy of charm and humor. Two people playing out a very vital game of love, an attractive fantasy with a precious tincture of truth to it."—N.Y. Times. ". . . perfectly charming entertainment, sexy, romantic and funny."—Women's Wear Daily.

*Royalty, $50—$35*

# WHO KILLED SANTA CLAUS?
## TERENCE FEELY
### (All Groups) Thriller
6 Men, 2 Women, Interior

Barbara Love is a popular television 'auntie'. It is Christmas, and a number of men connected with her are coming to a party. Her secretary, Connie, is also there. Before they arrive she is threatened by a disguised voice on her Ansaphone, and is sent a grotesque 'murdered' doll in a coffin, wearing a dress resembling one of her own. She calls the police, and a handsome detective arrives. Shortly afterwards her guests follow. It becomes apparent that one of those guests is planning to kill her. Or is it the strange young man who turns up unexpectedly, claiming to belong to the publicity department, but unknown to any of the others?

> ". . . is a thriller with heaps of suspense, surprises, and nattily cleaver turns and twists . . . Mr. Feeley is technically highly skilled in the artificial range of operations, and his dialogue is brilliantly effective."—The Stage. London.

*Royalty, $50—$25*

# A Breeze from The Gulf

## MART CROWLEY

## (Little Theatre) Drama

The author of "The Boys in the Band" takes us on a journey back to a small Mississippi town to watch a 15-year-old boy suffer through adolescence to adulthood and success as a writer. His mother is a frilly southern doll who has nothing to fall back on when her beauty fades. She develops headaches and other physical problems, while the asthmatic son turns to dolls and toys at an age when other boys are turning to sports. The traveling father becomes withdrawn, takes to drink; and mother takes to drugs to kill the pain of the remembrances of things past. She eventually ends in an asylum, and the father in his fumbling way tries to tell the son to live the life he must.

> "The boy is plunged into a world of suffering he didn't create. . . . One of the most electrifying plays I've seen in the past few years . . . Scenes boil and hiss . . . The dialogue goes straight to the heart." Reed, Sunday News.

*Royalty*, $50–$35

# ECHOES

## N. RICHARD NASH

## (All Groups) Drama
### 2 Men, 1 Woman, Interior

A young man and woman build a low-keyed paradise of happiness within an asylum, only to have it shattered by the intrusion of the outside world. The two characters search, at times agonizingly to determine the difference between illusion and reality. The effort is lightened at times by moments of shared love and "pretend" games, like decorating Christmas trees that are not really there. The theme of love, vulnerable to the surveillances of the asylum, and the ministrations of the psychiatrist, (a non-speaking part) seems as fragile in the constrained setting as it often is in the outside world.

> ". . . even with the tragic, sombre theme there is a note of hope and possible release and the situations presented specifically also have universal applications to give it strong effect . . . intellectual, but charged with emotion."—Reed.

*Royalty*, $50–$35

# VERONICA'S ROOM
## IRA LEVIN
### (Little Theatre) Mystery
### 2 Men, 2 Women, Interior

VERONICA'S ROOM is, in the words of one reviewer, "a chew-up-your-finger-nails thriller-chiller" in which "reality and fantasy are entwined in a totally absorbing spider web of who's-doing-what-to-whom." The heroine of the play is 20-year-old Susan Kerner, a Boston University student who, while dining in a restaurant with Larry Eastwood, a young lawyer, is accosted by a charming elderly Irish couple, Maureen and John Mackey (played on Broadway by Eileen Heckart and Arthur Kennedy). These two are overwhelmed by Susan's almost identical resemblance to Veronica Brabissant, a long-dead daughter of the family for whom they work. Susan and Larry accompany the Mackeys to the Brabissant mansion to see a picture of Veronica, and there, in Veronica's room, which has been preserved as a shrine to her memory, Susan is induced to impersonate Veronica for a few minutes in order to solace the only surviving Brabissant, Veronica's addled sister who lives in the past and believes that Veronica is alive and angry with her. "Just say you're not angry with her," Mrs. Mackey instructs Susan. "It'll be such a blessin' for her!" But once Susan is dressed in Veronica's clothes, and Larry has been escorted downstairs by the Mackeys, Susan finds herself locked in the room and locked in the role of Veronica. Or is she really Veronica, in the year 1935, pretending to be an imaginary Susan?

> The play's twists and turns are, in the words of another critic, "like finding yourself trapped in someone else's nightmare," and "the climax is as jarring as it is surprising." "Neat and elegant thriller."—*Village Voice*.

**ROYALTY, $50-$35**

# MY FAT FRIEND
## CHARLES LAURENCE
### (Little Theatre) Comedy
### 3 Men, 1 Woman, Interior

Vicky, who runs a bookshop in Hampstead, is a heavyweight. Inevitably she suffers, good-humouredly enough, the slings and arrows of the two characters who share the flat over the shop; a somewhat glum Scottish youth who works in an au pair capacity, and her lodger, a not-so-young homosexual. When a customer—a handsome bronzed man of thirty—seems attracted to her she resolves she will slim by hook or by crook. Aided by her two friends, hard exercise, diet and a graph, she manages to reduce to a stream-lined version of her former self—only to find that it was her rotundity that attracted the handsome book-buyer in the first place. When, on his return, he finds himself confronted by a sylph his disappointment is only too apparent. The newly slim Vicky is left alone once more, to be consoled (up to a point) by her effeminate lodger.

> "My fat Friend is abundant with laughs."—*Times Newsmagazine*. "If you want to laugh go."—*WCBS-TV*.

**ROYALTY, $50-$35**

#5

# PROMENADE, ALL!
## DAVID V. ROBISON

### (Little Theatre) Comedy
### 3 Men, 1 Woman, Interior

Four actors play four successive generations of the same family, as their business grows from manufacturing buttons to a conglomerate of international proportions (in the U.S. their perfume will be called Belle Nuit; but in Paris, Enchanted Evening). The Broadway cast included Richard Backus, Anne Jackson, Eli Wallach and Hume Cronyn. Miss Jackson performed as either mother or grandmother, as called for; and Cronyn and Wallach alternated as fathers and grandfathers; with Backus playing all the roles of youth. There are some excellent cameos to perform, such as the puritanical mother reading the Bible to her son without realizing the sexual innuendoes; or the 90-year-old patriarch who is agreeable to trying an experiment in sexology but is afraid of a heart attack.

> "So likeable; jolly and splendidly performed."—*N.Y. Daily News.* "The author has the ability to write amusing lines, and there are many of them."—*N.Y. Post.* "Gives strong, lively actors a chance for some healthy exercise. And what a time they have at it!"—*CBS-TV.*

### ROYALTY, $50-$35

.

# ACCOMMODATIONS
## NICK HALL

### (Little Theatre) Comedy
### 2 Men, 2 Women, Interior

Lee Schallert, housewife, feeling she may be missing out on something, leaves her husband, Bob, and her suburban home and moves into a two-room Greenwich Village apartment with two roommates. One roommate, Pat, is an aspiring actress, never out of characters or costumes, but, through an agency mix up, the other roommate is a serious, young, graduate student—male. The ensuing complications make a hysterical evening.

> "An amusing study of marital and human relations . . . a gem . . . It ranks as one of the funniest ever staged."—*Labor Herald.* "The audience at Limestone Valley Dinner Theater laughed at "Accommodations" until it hurt."—*News American.* "Superior theater, frivolous, perhaps, but nonetheless superior. It is light comedy at its best."—*The Sun, Baltimore.*

### ROYALTY, $50-$25